CLAIMED BY THE DESERT SHEIKH: DESERT KING, PREGNANT MISTRESS

Susan Stephens

MILLS & BOON

First published in Great Britain 2008
by Mills & Boon, an imprint of Harlequin (UK) Limited,
Large Print edition 2013
Harlequin (UK) Limited,
Eton House, 18-24 Paradise Road, Richmond, Surrey TW9 1SR

© Susan Stephens 2008

ISBN: 978 0 263 23615 6

Harlequin (UK) policy is to use papers that are natural, renewable and recyclable products and made from wood grown in sustainable forests. The logging and manufacturing process conform to the legal environmental regulations of the country of origin.

Printed and bound in Great Britain
by CPI Antony Rowe, Chippenham, Wiltshire

The ultimate kings of seduction!

THE PLAYBOYS
AND HEROES
COLLECTION

The Playboys and Heroes large print collection
gives you lavish stories of luxury
from your favourite top authors
in easier-to-read print.

Susan Stephens was a professional singer before meeting her husband on the tiny Mediterranean island of Malta. In true Modern™ Romance style they met on Monday, became engaged on Friday and were married three months after that. Almost thirty years and three children later, they are still in love. (Susan does not advise her children to return home one day with a similar story, as she may not take the news with the same fortitude as her own mother!)

Susan had written several non-fiction books when fate took a hand. At a charity costume ball there was an after-dinner auction. One of the lots, 'Spend a Day with an Author', had been donated by Mills & Boon author Penny Jordan. Susan's husband bought this lot, and Penny was to become not just a great friend but a wonderful mentor, who encouraged Susan to write romance.

Susan loves her family, her pets, her friends, and her writing. She enjoys entertaining, travel, and going to the theatre. She reads, cooks, and plays the piano to relax, and can occasionally be found throwing herself off mountains on a pair of skis or galloping through the countryside. Visit Susan's website: www.susanstephens.net—she loves to hear from her readers all around the world!

CHAPTER ONE

SHE was hiding in a rock pool, watching a naked man stride out of the surf. Beth Tracey Torrance, good girl, quiet girl, shop girl, Liverpool girl, pressed up against warm rocks in a foreign land beneath a blazing sun. And not just any country, but the desert kingdom of Q'Adar, where men rode camels and carried guns! Her stay-at-home self would say she was mad to be sitting here, frozen to the spot like one of the mannequins in the store—her friends would put it somewhat stronger—but she was drawn to this man. Just call it essential research. Well, she had to give a full report of her trip when she got back home, didn't she?

Beth leaned forward cautiously to take another look. If she'd thought the lash of sea on rock was elemental, the man leaving the ocean was even more stunning. Under different circumstances she would have turned away, because he was nude, but nothing seemed real to her here in Q'Adar—not the fabulous riches, the glamour, or the beautiful people.

Where was the camera when you needed it? With his lean, muscular frame and regal bearing, she was sure this man must be a member of the proud Q'Adaran race. And it wasn't every day you got the chance to stare at a man so beautiful he took your breath away.

Her colleagues at the luxury department store, Khalifa, would never believe this! She had amazed them once already with the news that her prize for being voted Shop Assistant of the Year for the Khalifa luxury group included not just a trip to the desert kingdom of Q'Adar, but a fairy-tale gown to wear to the Platinum and Diamond Ball—being held to celebrate the thirtieth birthday of the country's ruler, as well as his coronation, or whatever it was called when a man was voted Sheikh of Sheikhs. And this was the same man whose extensive business-portfolio included the Khalifa brand.

She had never met her boss, Mr Khalifa Kadir, the legendary founder of the international chain of luxury stores, but was stunned to think he would now be known as His Majesty. His full title was His Majesty Khalifa Kadir al Hassan, Sheikh of Sheikhs, Bringer of Light to His People. It sounded like something out of a fairy story, Beth thought as the man walked up the beach and disappeared behind some rocks.

And now she, Beth Tracey Torrance, was going to meet the Sheikh of Sheikhs when he handed her the trophy she'd won. So, should she bow or should she curtsey? Beth wondered, distractedly chewing her lip. There wasn't much room for manoeuvre in her tight-fitting dress, so maybe she should just make a small bow when she met him… *When she met him!* When she, an ordinary girl, met the Sheikh of Sheikhs! It was all she had dreamed about for weeks now. And yet that dream had just been eclipsed by some man on a beach.

Pressed back against the rocks, Beth closed her eyes and inwardly melted. Forget the sheikh. This man would be branded on her mind for ever!

He felt rather than saw the intruder. His training in the special forces had served him well. The sixth sense he had developed during army service had saved his life on several occasions, and had also proved a handy tool when it came to developing his business instinct. His profits now rivalled those of oil, and Q'Adar was rich in oil. Most sheikhs didn't work, but where was the challenge in spending oil wealth when that precious resource seeped out of the ground? And where was the satisfaction in paying experts to earn money for him? Where was the sense of achievement in sitting back while others did the work for him? He was always restless, always seeking the next challenge, and now he had accepted the greatest challenge of his life: to rescue his country, Q'Adar, from the brink of disaster.

Throwing back his head to embrace the warmth of the molten sun, the Sheikh of Sheikhs, His Majesty Khalifa Kadir al Hassan, rejoiced that he was more than strong enough for the task as he luxuriated in the seductive heat of his native land.

He was gorgeous, absolutely gorgeous. And if he'd just turn a little to the right...

No.

No!

What was she thinking?

Beth's thoughts flew into a frenzy as the man's naked body was fully revealed. She exhaled with relief as he turned his back. She didn't want him to turn around again or she'd be damaged for life. She'd never find his equal. *Never!* He'd been close enough for her to see *everything!* And there was an awful lot of everything to see. He wasn't even covered by a towel, though she could see one neatly folded on a rock. Thankfully the rock was some way away, which meant he wouldn't have to pass her hiding place when he went to get it. Which meant she was safe to go on staring at him. Well, she had to remember every bit of this in detail to tell her friends, didn't she?

To an untrained observer he might appear oblivious to the dangers around him, but he never took anything for granted, especially his personal safety. He had made his life outside Q'Adar, and was still weighing up the risks here. He had returned to his homeland at the request of the other sheikhs, who had asked him to lead them, and he was ready to serve. His life experiences had prepared him for most things—with the possible exception of the unfathomable workings of a woman's mind. His portfolio of business interests had achieved global renown, and he had no personal issues to distract him; no taint of scandal touched him. As a stranger, to emotion he doubted it ever would. His sense of duty was all-embracing, and, having accepted this challenge, he wouldn't let his fellow sheikhs down by carelessly offering himself up for slaughter.

As he moved steadily along the beach Khal caught sight of a flash of glowing hair. It confirmed his earlier analysis of the situation—the risk was small. An agent would have made her move by now. Paparazzi? The direction of the sun would have flared off their camera lens. No, this was a sight-seeing expedition by an amateur.

Burying his face in the towel he'd left ready for when he quit the sea, he took his time, knowing this would lull the young woman into a false sense of security. He could wait all he liked; she couldn't get past him. He was between her and the palace, and with the ocean in front of her, and thousands of miles of unseen desert surrounding them, she wouldn't be going anywhere.

Plus she would be growing increasingly un-

comfortable in the heat, while he felt refreshed—
and not just in the body, but in the mind; the sea
had cleansed him. He swam every day, either
in the pool at one of his many homes, or in the
ocean. It was one of his few indulgences. It allowed him to step outside himself—outside his
life. Pitting his strength against the ocean gave
him something else to think about other than balance sheets and treachery. He needed that space.
Q'Adar had grown fat and lazy in his absence,
and he intended to change that by setting up a
strong infrastructure and wiping out corruption.
It was a daunting task, and would take many
years to achieve, but eventually he would reach
that goal; he was determined to.

The fact that someone had managed to elude
his security guards was an example of the general sloppiness he had uncovered, though for now
good business-practice required him to hold back
on reprisal until he had a chance to assess all the
players involved. For what was a country, other
than a business to be managed efficiently for the
good of its people? It was ironic to think his business acumen was one of the reasons his fellow
sheikhs had voted him into this position of su-

preme power over them, but he didn't kid himself it had been a popularity poll—they knew his reputation. The financial press dubbed him ruthless and unforgiving, and where his employees were concerned that was correct. He didn't take the livelihoods of fifty-thousand people lightly. He defended them as sheikhs of old had defended their territories, and if that meant cutting out the dead wood, and neutralising the competition, then that was what he did.

But for now his interest lay in tracking down this young woman. He would use her as an example of how the security forces were deficient, and stealth was his weapon of choice. His angle of approach would make her think he was walking away from her, when in fact he would be coming closer with every step.

As he prowled closer he was forced to shut out the seductive beauty of his homeland. There was much in Q'Adar to tempt the senses, and it would be easy to slip into self-indulgent ways. A panorama of exquisite loveliness tempted him to lower his guard and linger. When he returned to the palace he would be greeted by sights of unimaginable splendour—every wall at the Palace of the Moon was decorated with gold leaf, and the doors were studded with precious stones. Beguiling perfumes would lure him into thinking of erotic pleasures, while music would thrum a constant siren-song through his senses.

The only sticking point for him at the palace was his mother. Hoping he would marry soon, she had assembled the world's most beautiful women for his perusal. Every royal house was represented—and there was no doubt her efforts had pleased the corrupt sheikhs, who didn't care about his choice of bedmate just so long as he was distracted and left them alone. What they had failed to realise was that his mistress was work, and that here in Q'Adar there was much to do.

Beth watched the man bury his face in the towel with a mixture of apprehension and fascination. There was something about his stillness that warned her to be wary. She couldn't shake off a feeling of uneasiness. Maybe he did know she was here, watching him. Maybe he wasn't just burying his face in a towel, but quietening his body in order to listen to his senses. As he lifted his head the onshore breeze caught his thick black hair and tossed it around his face. He was magnificent. She'd never seen anyone like him before, and she held her breath as he fixed the towel around his waist.

He started walking—thankfully, away from her. Cutting at right angles to the beach, he disappeared out of sight behind some more rocks...

Letting out her breath in a ragged stream, Beth relaxed. What an experience that had been! She wished there had been a sculpter on hand, or an artist, someone capable of capturing his likeness and sharing it with the world...

Beth shrieked as something cold and hard pressed into the back of her neck. *Was it a gun?* She was too frightened to turn and find out.

"Get up," a clipped male voice instructed. "Get up slowly, and turn around."

She did as he asked, stumbling in the sand, only to find the man on the beach confronting her. "I was told I would be safe here," she blurted out. "The new Sheikh has reserved this beach for his staff." Beth knew that she was rambling as tears of fright filled her eyes. She couldn't see the gun, but knew it must be somewhere. "I've got a permit..." No, she hadn't! She had changed out of her jeans into a sundress without pockets. "Don't you speak English?" she blurted, wondering if those few phrases were all he had.

"As well as you, I imagine," the man replied in a voice that was barely accented.

Beth found herself confronting the hardest, coldest eyes she'd ever seen, set in a face of savage beauty, but affront had taken the place of her anger. The man was twice her size, and much older than she was. She firmed her jaw. He had no need to threaten her with a gun. "Is it usual to intimidate guests to your country?"

She had guts, he'd give her that, but she had been spying on him, and she mustn't be allowed to think him an easy target. "Do you make a point of invading other people's privacy?" he snapped back.

Her cheeks turned an attractive shade of rose, telling him that emotion came easily to her. In that they were very different. But the moment of embarrassment swiftly passed, and now this barefoot intruder with her wind-tangled hair and flimsy beach-dress was shooting fire at him from crystal-blue eyes. She was much younger than he had first thought, and her skin had the texture of a downy peach. She was new to the unforgiving Arabian sun, and instinctively he took a step forward to back her into the shade.

"Don't you come near me!" she warned him, holding out her tiny hands to ward him off.

She was frightened, but still determined to put up a fight. And then he noticed that her small, straight nose had a sprinkling of freckles across the bridge…

Irrelevant. He was surprised that he'd noticed such a thing. Where had she come from, and how had she slipped past his guards? She wasn't part of his world or she would have been recognised him immediately. She must have drafted in to help with the celebrations. But, if that was the case, why was she sunning herself while everyone else was working? "Does your supervisor know you're here?"

"Does yours?"

He recoiled at her impudence. Then he recognised the accent. Natives of Liverpool weren't noted for holding back. "I asked the question first," he said evenly. "Have you considered the possibility that your supervisor might be worried about you?"

A crease appeared between her upswept taupe brows as she considered this. "It seems to me that yours has more cause to be worried about you."

"How do you work that out?" he said, deciding he would play along.

"Do they know you bring a gun to the beach?"

"A gun?" He had to hold back his astonishment as well as his amusement. Holding out his hands, palms flat, he showed her he had no weapons—concealed or otherwise—unless she felt like searching under his towel, of course. "I was merely attempting to attract your attention," he told her.

"Oh, I see," she said, catching on. "With one sea-cooled finger?" Her mouth firmed into an angry line. "So you don't use a gun, but you do assault guests to your country—well?" she demanded. "Don't I deserve the courtesy of a reply when you've frightened me half to death?"

He was still adapting to this radical change to the way people usually addressed him when his attention was drawn to her full rosebud-lips, and the difficulty she was having keeping them pressed flat in an expression of affront. He wanted to smile, because she was so young and so indignant, but he knew better than to prolong the encounter. "My apologies," he said mildly. As he spoke he touched his right hand to his breast and then to his forehead. "You are right to feel distress. As a visitor to my land you are of course my honoured guest…" As the silky words worked their ancient magic, he saw her eyes darken with more than interest. She wasn't so keen to get away now.

"Apology accepted," she said. "So, you work here too?"

Rather than answer he watched the flush rising on her cheeks. Her slight frame and pert breasts had made his senses stir. "That's right," he said at last. "I just got here."

"Oh, like me," she cut in, forgetting to be angry with him. "I expect you've come for the celebrations." She glanced towards the palace. "They told me a lot of new staff had been hired."

"Did they?"

She gave him a long, considering look, and then decided to trust him with a little more. "Q'Adar's the most beautiful country, isn't it?"

He could only agree. The sea was jade green with a white-lace frill, and his Palace of the Moon had turned rose pink in the mellow light of late afternoon.

"But it's not the flash that makes it so lovely, is it?" she demanded bluntly. "Though there's plenty of that around, from what I've seen. Thing is, ostentation's commonplace when you can see it on the telly any time you want."

"Ostentation?" He had thought the palace overblown when he'd returned to it after an absence too, but he wasn't sure how he felt about hearing criticism of it from a stranger.

"It's the scenery that gets you, isn't it?" she went on, gesturing around. "I think it's a combination of beach, sea, and the warmth of the people that makes Q'Adar so special."

She was making it increasingly hard for him to find fault with her, especially when she added, "I think it's the people most of all." She stopped then and blushed, and started fiddling with her hair, as if aware that she was keeping him. But then wariness shaded her eyes as she took on board the fact that she shouldn't be engrossed in conversation with a man she didn't know—a man who might even pose a danger to her...

"I won't hurt you," he said, lifting his hands.

She shrugged, a little defiant gesture to cover for the predicament in which she found herself, he guessed. And then a horn sounded somewhere in the palace, and she jumped. "What was that?" Still gasping for air, she stared at him for answers.

"That was the Nafir—"

"The what?"

"The Nafir," he said again. "It's a horn." He was finding it harder every moment to remain aloof from her infectious cheeriness. "It's a big horn about three metres long made of copper. It utters a single-note."

"That's not much use, then, is it?"

He drew himself up to his full height. "On the contrary. The Nafir is sounded on ceremonial occasions and will be played tonight to herald the start of the Sheikh's birthday."

"So that was a dress rehearsal?"

"I expect so."

She gave an exaggerated sigh. "Well, that's a relief! I was thinking *Walls of Jericho*—you know?

We wouldn't want that lot tumbling down on us, now, would we?" Hugging herself, she pulled a face as she stared up at the gigantic structure.

The Palace of the Moon had stood for centuries as a symbol of Q'Adar's pre-eminence in the Arab world, and he'd never heard anyone make light of it before. He didn't know what to make of this young woman—except, to say, she interested him. "Don't you think you should be getting back?" He was conscious that she must have duties, and he didn't want her to get in trouble.

"Shouldn't you?" Cocking her head, she levelled a cheeky stare at him.

"Oh, I'm all right for a bit longer."

"And so am I," she said. "There's ages to go before the ball."

"So you're a waitress?"

She laughed out loud. "Goodness me, no! Can you imagine it? Canapés flying everywhere and drinks all muddled up? I'd never be asked to do something like that!"

"So, you're a guest?"

"There's no need to sound quite so surprised," she scolded him. "Actually," she confided, touching his arm in her eagerness to make *him* feel at ease. "I'm halfway in between."

He felt her touch like a brand, and had to refocus to ask her, "Halfway in between what?"

"Halfway in between being a servant and a guest," she told him blithely. "I do work for the Sheikh, but I'm insignificant."

"Insignificant?" he queried. Of all the adjectives he might have used to describe this young woman, "insignificant" was not one of them. "I wouldn't call you that."

"That's very kind of you," she said sincerely. "But, I'd better tell you right away, I'm only a shop assistant."

"Only?" He thought about all the other sales assistants who worked for him at his luxury stores worldwide. They were the lifeblood of his business. He considered them to be the front line, and this girl was the best of them, he realised now as the mystery unravelled in front of him. "Tell me more," he said, wanting to hear her version of events.

"I won best Shop Assistant of the Year for the Khalifa group, and this is my prize," she said, gesturing around in a way he guessed was meant to encompass everything she had seen since arriving in Q'Adar.

"And do you like it?" She had already said she did, but he wanted to delve deeper into that quicksilver mind of hers.

"I love it. Who wouldn't? And they say the Sheikh's gorgeous!"

"Do they?" he said with surprise.

"I won't be able to pass an opinion on him until I see him tonight, but I'll let you know."

"Would you?" he said, containing his amusement. She was so very young, he was surprised when she leaned forward to confide in him.

"You know, I feel sorry for that sheikh…"

"Do you? Why?"

She stood back a pace, and her face turned solemn. "You probably think he's got everything, but a man like that is a hostage for life, isn't he?" And, without waiting for him to answer the question, she breezed on with concern. "He can never do what he wants, can he? He can only do what's right for everyone else."

He realised now that the inevitable question with its confident answer was part of her Liverpool charm. "Can't they be one and the same thing?" he said, marvelling at the fact that he was entering into a discussion with her. But, then, he couldn't believe he was standing here at all with a woman he didn't know.

She stood and thought about it for a while. "He'd have to be really strong to run a country, the Khalifa business, *and* find time for a private life."

"And you feel sorry for him?" He felt faintly affronted.

"Yes, I do," she said candidly.

Before he could argue with her premise, she shook her head. "It must be hideous, having people bow and scrape around you all day without knowing who to trust."

"Maybe the Sheikh is shrewder than you think."

Her face brightened. "I agree. He must be, mustn't he? Look what he's done with his business, for a start—and the other sheikhs wouldn't have voted him in if he wasn't exceptional. I like that, don't you?" she demanded without pausing for breath.

"What do you mean?"

"The way all the other sheikhs voted for him. And, of course, we couldn't be more thrilled back home that it's *our* sheikh that's going to be the ruler of Q'Adar. Except we're all worried now that he might sell off the Khalifa stores."

"Why would he do that?"

"He might lose interest in business when he has the running of a country on his mind."

"There's no danger of that."

"You sound very sure." Interest coloured her voice. "You have the inside track, don't you?" And, when he didn't answer, she pressed him eagerly. "You're someone important, aren't you?"

"I hear things on the palace grapevine," he explained with a dismissive gesture.

"Of course you do—and it's the same for us back at the store. We always get to hear what's going on. What he's like?" she said after a moment's pause.

"The Sheikh?"

"You must know him if you work for him. I was off with flu last time he visited Khalifa in Liverpool, worse luck. Is he stern?"

"Very."

"He's not mean to you, is he?"

"We have a good working relationship," he reassured her.

"Oh, well, I'd better get a move on," she said, heading off in the direction of the palace. "Thanks for the chat. Are you coming?" she said, turning to face him. "Only, I have to go now and put my glad rags on."

"For the Platinum and Diamond Ball? Of course…" He had almost forgotten. He had allowed himself to be distracted by a pair of slender legs showing their first hint of tan, along with fine-boned hips and a hand-span waist. The unaffected friendliness in the young girl's eyes was so refreshing, he allowed himself another moment's indulgence. "Are you looking forward to the ball, Cinderella?"

Her face turned serious. "Don't call me that. I'm not Cinderella; my name is Beth. Beth Tracey Torrance." And then, taking him completely by surprise, she held out her tiny hand for him to shake. "And I'm not waiting around for some fairy godmother to come and save me. I make my own luck."

"Do you indeed?" he said, releasing her hand, which was soft and cool in spite of the heat, and delivered a surprisingly firm handshake. "And how do you go about that?"

"Hard work," she said frankly. "I read something once written by Thomas Edison. You know—the light-bulb man? I've never forgotten it, and it's become my motto."

"Go on…" His lips were threatening rebellion, but he managed somehow to control them and confine himself to a brief nod of encouragement.

"Thomas Edison said, 'opportunity is missed by most people because it comes dressed in overalls and looks like work'."

"And you agree with that?"

"Yes." She drew the word out, as well as up and down the vocal register, for even more emphasis. "It's worked for me. But then I love my work."

"You do?"

"I love people," she said, eyes gleaming with enthusiasm. "I love seeing their faces when I find something in the store that's going to make a difference to their lives. Maybe it's a gift, or a treat they're buying for themselves—it doesn't matter. I just want to see *the look* transform their faces…"

And now her face was transformed with a smile. "So *the look*'s your secret of success?"

"Oh, there are others on the floor just as good

as me," she told him. "Sales figures are all a matter of luck, aren't they?"

After what she'd told him, he very much doubted it. The horn sounded again, and this time she didn't jump. "Isn't this romantic?" she said instead.

They both gazed up at the towering ramparts, where pennants were being raised in his honour. The sun had sunk low enough to turn the walls of his citadel a soft shade of rose madder, which, yes, he supposed could be called romantic by those with a vivid imagination and time enough to look.

"Imagine having this much fuss made of your birthday," she said, drawing his attention again. "I thought I was lucky, but—"

"Lucky?" he interrupted, wanting to know more about her.

"I have the best family on earth," she assured him passionately. As she laughed, he presumed all the happy reminiscences must be flooding in. "They do all sorts of batty things for me on my birthday. Wonderful surprises…" Her eyes turned dreamy. "You know the type of thing?"

Actually, no, he didn't. His parents loved him,

but duty had always coloured his life. There had been little time to party, and much to learn. If he hadn't been voted Sheikh of Sheikhs, he would still have returned to Q'Adar to serve his people at some point.

"I expect the Sheikh's up there now," she said, shading her eyes as she gazed up to where the bursting flames of the dipping sun were reflected in the windows. "There'll be champagne corks popping right now, I'll bet."

They would be anxiously awaiting his return. He had been gone for far too long. The plans for this celebration had been rigorously planned minute by minute, and unlike the celebrations she had described there would be no surprises. The Platinum and Diamond Ball would not conform to any of the wacky images Beth had conjured, but would be stiff with ceremony, and fraught with pitfalls, especially for an innocent like Beth Tracey Torrance. "Is someone taking care of you tonight at the ball?"

"Taking care of me?" she slanted him a coquettish look. "Why? Are you offering? Because, if you are, I think it's time you told me your name."

"I'll be working," he reminded her.

"Oh, don't worry," she said, flipping her wrist. "I was only teasing you. I know you must have lots to do, and most probably hundreds of gorgeous women in your harem—" Her hand flew to cover her mouth. "Sorry! *Sorry!*" She looked mortified, and her accent broadened as she exclaimed in horror, "I didn't mean that! I hate stereotypes, don't you?"

"No offence taken," he assured her. "And, as for my name, you can call me Khal…"

"Khal as in *Khalifa*?" she interrupted. "Now, that *is* a coincidence…" As she stared at him her face changed and grew pale beneath its scattering of freckles. "No, it isn't, is it?" she said.

CHAPTER TWO

THREE things happened in quick succession. His bodyguards appeared out of nowhere, Beth screamed as one of them shoved a gun in her face, and he launched himself in her defence, seizing the gun so fast the man reeled back. "Leave her!" he commanded in a shout.

Beth's face was twisted with fear as he reached out to reassure her. His men had stormed in—using unnecessary force to make up for their earlier negligence, he deduced—but Beth was young and a stranger to violence, and they had terrified her. "Come," he said, beckoning her closer with his outstretched hand.

Shaking her head, she refused to look at him. He sensed her fear, but above that he sensed her determination to maintain control. Even so, inwardly he gave a curse directed at his men. She had been so full of life only moments before, and now that life had been crushed out of her. She had been like a breath of fresh air, but her innocence had been trampled. She had come to Q'Adar with some romantic notion of what life would be like in a desert kingdom, and couldn't be expected to understand the harsh realities. He lost no time dismissing his men, and then asked her, "Will you walk back to the palace with me, Beth?"

Hugging herself, she shook her head. He couldn't blame her for feeling the way she did when the ugly threat of violence was still hanging in the air. It would be so alien to anything she was used to, she'd have no coping strategies.

"Is that how it is here?" she said at last.

He was surprised to see her clear blue gaze had turned to steel.

"If you mean the guards—"

"And the guns."

"They are a necessary precaution."

"To protect you from your people?" Pressing her lips down, she shook her head in disapproval. "Then I really do feel sorry for you…" Still hugging herself, she stalked away.

He had pulled her CV from the pile and was studying it in the bath, allowing the eucalyptus-scented steam to clear his head. Beth certainly had the gift when it came to selling, and along with the bare facts he found several glowing references—not just from her line manager, but from her colleagues too. They said if she had a fault it was that Beth Torrance didn't know how good she was...

He smiled as he thought about this, about Beth—and he rarely smiled, because life was a serious business. She was so unspoiled, but then she was only twenty-two... Yet she was confident enough to stand her ground and fight for what she believed in. The Sheikh and the shop girl were as one in that, he reflected wryly.

He turned back to the folder to look at her reports from school, where she'd captained the hockey team and led the first-aid group, generally showing a solid performance in all her academic studies. From school she had moved straight into a management-training course with Khalifa, which involved working in every department over the course of five years, and was not an easy option. Her reason for doing this, he read, smiling again as he imagined her writing it, was because she had wanted "to get stuck into something right away". She didn't mince her words.

Beth Tracey Torrance, aged twenty-two, might be a small problem in the scale of things he had to deal with, but he wasn't about to set her adrift in a sea of sharks. Calling up his mother, the Dowager Sheikha, he asked for one of her trusted attendants to be assigned to their visitor. "She's a young girl in a foreign land, and we must ensure that her stay is—" he chose his next words with care "—comfortable and safe." Ignoring the suspicion in his mother's voice, he ended the call.

The young girl sent to help Beth dress for the ball was a good listener. Beth was still fretting as she helped her with her make-up. What would her friends say when she went back to Khalifa and they realised she'd let them down? "I promised them all I'd put the trophy in the staff lounge," she explained as the young girl pinned a fresh orchid in her hair. "I wanted everyone to share it. But now I won't have a trophy to put there, will I? The Sheikh will never give it to me now..."

The girl shook her head.

"Well, it's no use looking on the black side, is

it? I'd better get that dress on because, trophy or no trophy, I am going to that ball." At least if she attended the ball she'd have something to share with her colleagues, Beth thought, feeling nervous as she thought about it. None of this had seemed real while she had been chatting away— not this magnificent suite of rooms in the Palace of the Moon, or the beach with the man on it, or the guns... But now it did, and she had to go to the ball all alone.

When she got up from the stool, and looked at the silvery ball-gown shimmering on its hanger next to the dressing gown she'd just discarded, her heart went wild. But she wasn't going to turn tail and run, Beth determined, though that was exactly what she felt like doing. No. She was going to this ball, and she was going to face up to the amazingly glamorous and stunningly endowed Sheikh—and if there was even the smallest chance that she could come away with that trophy then she would. "Could you help me, please?" she said, knowing she couldn't fasten the dress unaided. As the girl passed her the dressing gown, Beth, still thinking distractedly about Khal, said, "No, I meant the dress—" But then she noticed the girl had blushed a deep shade of red, and the penny finally dropped. "You don't speak English, do you?"

"I am *sorree*," the young girl managed in a halting accent.

"No, I'm the one who should be sorry," Beth argued. "Rabbiting on like that and you not understanding a word of it. And that's not the first mistake I've made today—if only!" Beth exclaimed, pulling a face with a laugh. "Come on," she said, smiling as she put her arm around the other girl's shoulders. "Let's do this together."

Taking the dress down from the padded hanger, Beth handed it to the maid. "You've done me a favour, you have. You've woken me up—and about time too! It's time to put my foreign-travel head on and snap out of this. 'Ooh, the sun's shining, and I left my brain behind in Liverpool'. Don't worry if you didn't understand a word of that," she added, giving the startled girl a hug. "You didn't miss much—and that's a whole lot more than can be said for me!"

Beth grimaced as she caught sight of herself clattering along the fabulous corridor in her five-inch heels. There were floor-to-ceiling mirrors set into the golden walls, so there was no escaping the truth. No escaping her bodyguard, either! They had sent a fierce-looking woman to collect her. Did she wear a gun too? Beth wondered as she struggled to keep up. Shoes that had seemed such a good idea back at the store were killing her now. She might be short, but she always wore flats so she could scoot around finding things for her customers. Heels this high demanded the skill of a tightrope walker—skill she definitely didn't possess. "Can you slow down a bit, please?" she begged as her stern-looking companion put on a spurt of speed.

The woman didn't answer, and as she had introduced herself as one of the Dowager Sheikha's personal attendants Beth thought she had better not push it. Personal *scary person*, Beth decided—definitely not someone you'd want to get on the wrong side of. The woman couldn't have made it clearer that she was used to escorting royalty.

"While I feel like a chicken in a bandage," Beth muttered, using her head to propel herself along. Graceful didn't come in to it. Majestic? Forget it. She was a shop assistant at the palace under sufferance, and the Sheikha's attendant wasn't going to let her forget it any time soon.

The pace they were walking at made Beth's heart beat even faster. Her hair had started to fall down, and fronds of it were sticking to her face. As if that wasn't bad enough, she had chatted up the Sheikh of Sheikhs as if he were a beach boy. *And* she had seen him naked! What would the Dowager Sheikha make of that? How was she supposed to look at His Majesty now? What if she couldn't control herself? What if she started giggling?

As they stopped in front of two gigantic doors, men dressed in flowing robes opened them. Beth acknowledged them both with a smile and a cheery greeting, which only brought a stony look of disapproval to her chaperon's face. That was the least of Beth's worries. The ballroom was crowded, and was she imagining it or had it gone utterly silent at the sight of her? No, she wasn't imagining it. Everyone had turned to stare. There must be spies everywhere in a palace, Beth thought, noticing servants whispering together. This was a real international gathering with "high and mighties" from every land, and enough diamonds flashing to sink a ship. Had one of these people seen her on the beach with the Sheikh, or had their servants reported her? Did they think there was an ulterior motive to her being here? Did they think her win was a fix, just a ruse, to bring her to Q'Adar so the Sheikh could enjoy her?

Beth shivered at the thought of what must be going through people's minds. But as the woman swept ahead of her she knew she must pull herself together fast. Tossing back her ruined hair, she firmed her jaw, sending the fresh flower the maid had so carefully fixed tumbling over her eye. She brushed it back and tipped her chin, and started forward again. Beth couldn't know that a keen black gaze was fixed on her with interest from behind a gilded screen.

She had been sitting at a dark table in a forgotten corner of the ballroom for nearly an hour. And she wanted to chat with someone. She didn't want to be stuck away like this, like last week's dirty washing, as if she was something to put out of the way and forget—and with the Dowager's

Sheikha's sidekick glaring at her if she so much as crossed her legs. She *needed* to chat. If she was going to work off her nerves, she needed to move about. Why had they invited her if the organisers couldn't even be bothered to check up on her and see that she was okay? She would have arranged things differently in Liverpool—everyone would have got a proper welcome.

As yet another waiter studiously ignored her Beth decided enough was enough; she was parched, and if she didn't have a glass of water soon… She was not going to sit here a moment longer and be ignored. She was an ambassador too—for the Khalifa stores—and as such she had no intention of hiding in the shadows feeling sorry for herself.

Beth would have carried off her intentions brilliantly had she been accustomed to wearing five-inch heels, but as it was she tripped at the edge of the dance floor, right in front of an amazingly tall and pretty princess. At least, Beth assumed the girl *must* be a princess, judging by the group of people standing around her tutting, and the fact that Beth was blinded by diamonds when she looked up. "I'm so sorry…" She tried scrambling to her feet, but only made it to all fours with her rump sticking high in the air because her stiletto heels stubbornly refused to find purchase on the marble floor. Meanwhile the princess and her attendants skirted round her, as if she was a dog's doodle, before sweeping off. It took a young girl who had been watching all this to help her to her feet.

"Thank you," Beth said gratefully, brushing herself down as the girl steadied her.

"Are you sure you're all right? You're more than welcome to join us at our table..." The girl pointed to where a group of young people were sitting. "We've been watching you," she admitted. "We hated the way everyone stared at you when you came in—"

"Don't worry about me," Beth said, pretending her nose wasn't stinging with the threat of tears. "I'm fine..." I can do this, she was thinking, though her ballgown was ripped now, and the flower from her hair was lying crushed on the floor. "But thank you for coming over to help me," she said, finding her customary grin.

"Well, if you change your mind...?"

"I'll remember," Beth promised. "And thank you, again..." Composing herself, she looked around, and this time no one returned her gaze. It was as if she had become invisible. No one wanted to get involved with a nobody, Beth gathered, except for her new friend. They shared a smile before the girl sat down again with her companions.

Blowing the hair out of her eyes, Beth wondered what to do for a moment, and then decided that watching would probably teach her more than anything. Her first thought was that the scent of wealth was stifling, and she could tell that Khal's guests had really gone to town on the platinum-and-diamond theme of the ball. But strip all the glitz and glitter away and they were just people the same as she was, probably with many of the same worries and concerns. At least that was what she thought, until she noticed people talking behind their hands and jostling for position in the final minutes before Khal arrived. Some of the women were licking their bottom lip and adjusting their dress to show more cleavage in preparation for His Majesty's arrival—which made weird feelings jostle inside her, almost as if she was feeling protective of Khal.

Which she did, Beth realised. What did Khal

see in all this? What did it mean? What did it add up to? As far as she could tell everyone was after him for something, and this ball was just another opportunity for people to advance themselves.

Being an outsider, even of this shallow group, wasn't nice. There was only one table where people were having fun for its own sake, as far as Beth could see and that was the table where the young girl who had rescued her was sitting. Beth wished now that she had accepted the invitation to go and sit with them. As it was, she felt like leaving to start packing for her return home. But she wouldn't, because she was here to represent her colleagues at the Khalifa stores. She would hold her head up high and remember that the owner of those stores might be the Sheikh of Sheikhs in Q'Adar, but he was also her boss—as well as the driving force behind the Khalifa brand—and this employee had no intention of letting Khal or her co-workers down.

CHAPTER THREE

HAVING surveyed the ballroom from his private viewing-area and seen what he wanted to, he dismissed his entourage and walked alone in the gardens. He always centred himself before an appearance, and tonight he craved that inner calm more than ever. Because he had allowed himself to be distracted by some young girl newly arrived from England, and however hard he tried to concentrate his thoughts kept returning to Beth Tracey Torrance.

She was more than the breath of fresh air he'd first thought her, much more. He might have known she would turn up to receive her trophy in spite of her embarrassment at the beach. He'd even had to admit to a rush of pleasure when he spotted her—as if emotion of any kind was possible for the ruler of Q'Adar. But Beth was a one-off, an original, and she had made him smile. She was plucky and unsophisticated, and completely untutored in the ways of the world. His lips tugged harder when he pictured her marching away from him. Who did that? Who ever turned their back on him? For all her youth and innocence her passions ran to the extreme, and she wasn't afraid to show them, which was a novelty. But now he must put her out of his mind. He was about to put on a show of strength, and couldn't be distracted by thoughts of relationships for which he had no time. If and when he formed an alliance some time in the future, it would be with someone from a similar background, someone who understood the pressures of royal life, and who had been schooled in that role since birth. That certain someone would have to possess the confidence to appear regal and unflustered at his side in every situation.

But would he ever get that picture of Beth Tracey Torrance and her cheeky smile out of his head? He couldn't forget the way she had turned her head to look at him while the onshore breeze had played with her shimmering hair. Nor would he forget those full lips, and how they firmed, or the crystal-blue eyes that could so quickly turn to ice if he said something she disapproved of.

He would like to soften those lips and turn that ice to fire, but he had to put those thoughts out of his head now because duty was calling him and he had to go.

Beth was still standing at the scene of her embarrassment when the orchestra quietened and a hush fell over the room. As all the elegant couples on the dance floor began to make their way back to their seats, she used the crush of perfumed flesh to escape the beady eye of the Sheikha's attendant and cross to the table of young guests where her friend was sitting. There was no point in remaining stubbornly alone. They had asked her to join them, and she'd have more to tell her friends that way.

As Beth had hoped the table of young people welcomed her, and quickly drew her into their conversation. They were an international group, Beth soon discovered, who had been to school in England and had only recently been summoned back to Q'Adar by their families to show support for the new leader.

"This is it!" Jamilah, the young girl who had

rescued Beth, excitedly informed her. "The Sheikh will be here any minute..."

As Beth nodded her throat dried and her heart went crazy. A fanfare of trumpets announced the opening of the golden doors. Even the most seasoned diplomat and jaded royal was riveted, she noticed, and no wonder. Surely none of them had ever seen such splendour before? But then Beth smiled secretly to herself, remembering that the boss of the world's most prestigious chain of luxury stores would know a thing or two about presentation.

As the lights in the ballroom dimmed, the spotlight on the golden doors grew brighter. Into this pool of light strode a tall, imposing figure clad in flowing black robes which were heavily embroidered with gold thread. "The master of ceremonies," Beth's neighbour discreetly informed her.

The man dressed in his robes of office stood for a moment before walking deeper into the hall. The stream of light followed him, and at his signal it widened to encompass the entire dance floor. Onto this stage strode four musicians, carrying slim golden trumpets. They wore the crimson, black and gold livery of Khalifa, with the black hawk, that was the personal symbol of Khalifa Kadir al Hassan, prominently displayed. The same image was shown on the tasselled flags falling from their instruments, and as they raised them to their lips the hawks undulated as if the Sheikh's birds of prey were indeed flying.

The musicians" cheeks filled, and a silver sound cut the silence. It echoed on and on, and as it died away a party of stately men entered on silent, sandaled feet. Their robes fluttered as they lined up against the jewelled walls. Beth guessed these must be the senior members of the royal council, and she thought them a magnificent sight. Some were wearing belts studded with lapis lazuli that glinted as they walked, while others had golden scimitars flashing at their side, and a few had links attached to the belts at their waist from which dropped their keys of office. But for all their grandeur these powerful men formed up like a flock of well-trained doves to await their Sheikh of Sheikhs.

Beth's heart swelled with pride at the thought that, wherever in the world the Khalifa name appeared, it reigned supreme, and she could hardly wait to see what came next. And this time the surprise was even greater. Everyone gasped as a youth galloped into the arena on a fiery stallion, and, though Beth thought him nowhere near as imposing as his master, there was no doubt that his horsemanship was outstanding. As he brought the stallion to a skidding halt he surveyed the audience, while his mount's polished hooves pawed the floor. He was carrying a small bright bugle, and, urging his horse to rear up, he sounded it. This was a signal for a band of horsemen to join him. Each of them was mounted on a magnificent Arab stallion, and all wore the black howlis around their heads, which covered their faces so that just their fierce black eyes showed beneath the folds of cloth. Long knives glinted at their waist, and their manner spoke of a warrior past and an allegiance to their new leader. Beth's heart was thundering painfully as she watched them bring their restless horses in line, and now there was only the sound of the animals snorting and their bridles chinking as a deep hush fell over the ballroom.

It was into this silent assembly he came, towering over every other man in the room, and proving that he had no need of personal show, or horse, or even fanfare to herald his arrival. His Majesty Khalifa Kadir al Hassan, Sheikh of Sheikhs, Bringer of Light to his People, had the power to command attention with his presence alone. And as his gaze swept the room everyone rose to their feet

Except for Beth, who remained frozen to the spot. Seeing Khal like this had sent her heart-rate off the scale. Dressed in the simple robes of a Bedouin warrior he needed neither gold nor weaponry to stamp his authority on the room. Power flowed from him, caressing her with the promise of his strength and virility, and, back-lit like this, his magnificently toned form was clearly visible beneath his fluid robes. It would take a very foolish man indeed to challenge Khal's right to the title Sheikh of Sheikhs, Beth thought, longing for him to look at her. He was the man every woman would want for their lover, the man they would crave for their protector, the father of their child.

And this was not the time for daydreams, she told herself sensibly. But how hard was it to be sensible when your imagination was running riot?

More than anything Beth had always wanted a

family of her own; the family she always talked about was a fiction she used to make her feel she belonged. She realised now she was secretly on the lookout for the ideal man—and, though she'd found him, her daydreams involving Beth Tracey Torrance and the Sheikh of Sheikhs was just another fiction. A man like Khal would marry for the good of the state and the benefit of his people; love wouldn't come into it. She only had to watch the other women reacting to him to know that. They all wanted Khal, and eventually he would choose one of them. He certainly wouldn't be taking his chances with Beth Tracey Torrance from Liverpool!

"Khalifa Kadir al Hassan…" Beth sighed, then jerked alert, realising Khal's name was in her head because the herald had just introduced his master to the assembled guests, and that everyone was standing. Except for her! She almost knocked her chair over as she quickly remedied the situation.

He saw her at once, and not just because she was the only person in the ballroom who didn't rise the moment he entered the room. He saw her because they seemed joined by some invisible thread. And that was not just inconvenient, it was a situation that could not be allowed to continue. If the only way to deal with it was to see Beth privately so he could reassure himself that she was an unsuitable distraction, then that was what he would do.

He turned from her. It was time to forgot Beth Torrance and concentrate his powers of intuition on everyone else attending the ball. In a country enduring birth-pangs, there were always those who would stand in the way of progress so they could hold on to their old, corrupt ways, and it was these people he intended to root out. But each time his gaze raked the hall it found Beth.

He'd looked at her. He had. She wasn't imagining it! The Sheikh of Sheikhs had remembered her and had looked at her. At least he hadn't forgotten her. Beth Tracey Torrance had made an impression on a sheikh! She couldn't wait to tell her friends.

But then Beth started fretting. Was it the fact that she had turned her back on him on the beach and stalked away that made him remember her?

Maybe she shouldn't be feeling quite so thrilled—maybe he had a dungeon waiting. And she didn't have her hands on that trophy yet—the trophy she had promised her friends she wouldn't return home without. But, if the ruler of Q'Adar forgave her and went ahead with the presentation, she'd have to say something and look at him, and that was almost worse.

She'd just have to make sure she didn't blurt out something completely inappropriate, Beth thought, starting to panic. She definitely mustn't say, "I hardly recognised you in your clothes." Biting her lip as she settled back in her seat, Beth told herself to relax and concentrate on the speeches.

His good intentions were shot to hell. Try as he might to focus on the speeches, all he could think about was Beth Tracey Torrance and the fact that she was staring at him. He should have her taken away and locked her up for her own safety. He realised now that everyone else was paying close attention to the proceedings, and just the two of them were distracted by each other. And now it was his turn to speak. He made it short and sweet, and when it was time for everyone to stand and bow before him he signalled more impatiently than he had intended that they must sit down again. He blamed Beth. He needed her out of his eye-line.

Beth gave a little jump as a cheer went up, and then realised that the Sheikh of Sheikhs" guards of honour had raised their weapons in a salute to him and were roaring their approval. And she hadn't even noticed them walk in. She had been too distracted by their leader. And how he had looked at her. She wasn't imagining it. And that look was well worth a night in the dungeon—for the ruler of Q'Adar stood centre-stage, backlit as if by Hollywood, with testosterone flying off him like sparks from a Catherine wheel. In this land of fierce, hard men, His Majesty Khalifa Kadir al Hassan was the hardest of them all. And she wanted him like mad, Beth confided to her inner self, glancing round guiltily in case there were any mind readers on her table. Who was she to look at their sheikh? Except to say that she knew another side of their ruler—the boss of the Khalifa group ran a company that held the best record for pastoral care of its employees in the world.

Which was why she was here. The trophy was just another example of how highly Khalifa Kadir regarded his employees. Thought it was hard to credit him with any gentleness now, when he appeared to be everything a warrior sheikh should be and more.

He was aware of her every second. Seated on the raised dais with the other members of the royal family, he told himself that this distraction was nothing more than his natural concern for an innocent abroad. He wanted to be sure Beth was safe; of course he did. He was concerned that the attendant his mother had sent at his request to look after Beth had abandoned her when she'd joined the table of young people. Beth worked for him, and therefore Beth was his responsibility.

Beth. Beth… She had eaten up too much of his time already. His body's responses to her were nothing more than an adrenalin rush brought on by this occasion. The fact that he could feel her clear blue gaze burning into him meant nothing. She was looking at him so she could report to her friends back home, and that was all. She would report that she had stared boldly at the Sheikh, and that he had stared back at her.

She was over-excited and needed to calm down. Beth gazed longingly at the exit. The girl seated next to her took her chance to ask if they could swap plates. Beth had hardly touched her food, and the chocolate pudding did look delicious, she noticed now it was too late. "You can have it," she said, smiling. She knew that feeling—the hole in the stomach that only chocolate could fill.

"Sure?"

"Positive." Beth tore her glance from the Sheikh, welcoming the distraction. "I'm overwhelmed," she admitted, exchanging plates. "I can't face eating. It isn't every day I find myself in a place like this."

"Lucky you!" the girl exclaimed, laughing. "Imagine having to dress like this on a regular basis." Coming closer, she confided, "I'd far rather be galloping across the desert."

"Wish I could," Beth agreed, thinking how romantic that sounded.

"You will if you stay here for very long," her

new friend promised, forking up a mouthful of cake.

"I'm going home soon," Beth explained.

"Then you'll just have to come back, won't you? Oh, look!" Beth's new friend exclaimed, swallowing hectically. "I think they're calling you." Grabbing Beth's arm, she drew her attention to a stern-looking man, dressed in the royal livery, who was beckoning to Beth in a stiff and impatient manner. "You didn't tell me you were someone special!" she exclaimed again.

"I can assure you, I'm not," Beth said, shaking her head wryly.

"Well, good luck anyway." The young girl touched her arm.

"Thank you. I'm going to need it!"

"So, that's your little shop girl," Khal's mother commented as Beth approached. "She's a pretty little thing, but I'm sure she's feeling quite disorientated here. Why don't I go and reassure her?"

"You, Mother?" Khal's eyes narrowed. His mother would let nothing and no one stand in the way of her ambitions for her one remaining child. He had never been under her thumb, but it worried him that her sights might be set on Beth now. He couldn't expect Beth to know how to handle his mother, and he half rose from his seat in order to intercept the Dowager Sheikha.

"You seem to have forgotten, Khal," his mother said, waiting impatiently for him to move aside. "That I was a no-one when I came to this country; I know how it feels to be a stranger in a foreign land."

He had not forgotten, but he wondered at her mention of it. "Beth's flight home is already booked."

"Beth?" His mother gave him a long, searching look.

"Mother," he murmured, leaning close. "You're not as subtle as I remember."

"That's because I'm growing more desperate, my son. I want you to find a bride and settle down."

"Is that why you invited every eligible female you could find to decorate these celebrations?" And when she lifted her chin and refused to answer him he added, "I may indeed settle one day, Mother, but I will never settle for second best."

"Like a shop girl?" His mother stared at him keenly.

"Are you worried about Beth?" He laughed it off. "I promise you, you will have the grandchildren you long for—just not yet." Having seen his mother comfortably settled again, he raised her jewelled hand to his lips.

"I love you, Khalifa." His mother stared into his eyes. "Which means I only want the best for you."

"I love you too, but I despair when you're fooled by gilt and tinsel..." He gave a meaningful glance at the row of compliant princesses all leaning forward in an attempt to attract his attention. "I'll find a bride in my own time," he assured his mother. "And now, if you will excuse me...?"

His mother didn't attempt to impose her will on him a second time, and he was just gathering his robes around him in preparation to return to his seat when a shriek made him turn. There had been a collision at the foot of the stairs. Some clumsy oaf had spilled a tray of drinks over Beth, and now her ballgown was ruined. Beth had frozen and was uncertain what to do.

"Shall I remain seated, my son?" his mother

whispered at his ear. "Or would you have me go to her and help her?"

He ground his jaw in frustration. It would have suited him better to keep the two of them apart.

"You can hardly be the one to usher her out of the hall and have her return some time later in a new dress, now, can you?" his mother pointed out.

"I'm not sure what you're suggesting," he told her with matching guile. "But I can assure you I am above gossip, Mother."

"But Beth's reputation would be ruined."

His lips tugged in wry defeat as his mother arched her brows.

"Let me go to her, Khalifa, and I promise to bring her back to you unharmed..."

He weighed the facts. Beth's misery had only increased as she'd attempted to scrub at the stains with a napkin someone had handed her. Her evening was on the point of ruin. "Go to her, and be sure that you do bring her back to me unharmed. Be gentle with her," he stressed, standing aside to allow his mother and her attendants to pass. "And please remember that Beth has a trophy to collect, so don't keep her long. She must receive her award before the festivities can begin."

"If you ask me," his mother murmured dryly on her way past him, "the fun has already started."

He feared for Beth as he watched his mother descending like a galleon in full sail, with her flotilla of hard-nosed females in close formation behind. But somehow he thought Beth would cope, and either way his mother was doing him a favour taking Beth out of his sight. Beth Tracey Torrance had proved far too much of a distraction as it was.

CHAPTER FOUR

"THANK YOU, Your Majesty. This is really too good of you!" Beth exclaimed, blushing furiously as she sank into the first proper curtsey of her life. The Sheikha had brought her into a part of the palace Beth had never thought to see, the Dowager Sheikha's private apartment, and now they were surrounded by silks, satins and French perfume, in the most sumptuous lace-trimmed room. Unfortunately she spoiled the moment as she made her curtsey when the seams of the ruined dress finally gave way.

The Sheikha, to her credit, appeared not to notice the ugly ripping sound.

"Nonsense!" she exclaimed with a flick of her wrist. "Any friend of my son's—"

"Oh, we're not friends," Beth blurted frankly, her cheeks turning hotter still when she heard the chorus of disapproving clucks rising from the Sheikha's attendants because she had interrupted the royal personage. "I mean, your son's my boss, and that's all."

"Your *boss*?" The Dowager Sheikha said, savouring the word.

Okay, so maybe she had protested a tad too heartily, Beth thought, hurrying to explain. "That's right. We hadn't even met until today. I was away last time he called at the store. I'd never seen him before we ran into each other at the beach."

"On the beach? You met my son at the beach?"

So the Sheikha was aware Khal swam naked. Could her cheeks grow any hotter? Beth wondered. "I didn't look at him. I mean...I didn't stare..."

"I should hope not," the Sheikha agreed, delicately dabbing at her nose with a fine lace-handkerchief.

"And we barely spoke at all," Beth hurried to reassure her, but Khal's mother had already turned away, hiding who knew what thoughts.

"Bring out the star dress," the Dowager Sheikha commanded, turning from her.

Beth's glance flicked from attendant to attendant as they gasped, but when she saw the gown the Sheikha had chosen for her to wear she thought she understood why they were astounded. It was stunning, and must have cost a fortune. "Oh, I couldn't," she gasped, unable to tear her eyes away from a dream of a dress shimmering in the light. Composed of silver chiffon, it was embroidered over every inch with tiny diamanté stars.

"You think it a little old-fashioned?" Khal's mother demanded.

"Oh no, I love it," Beth's said impulsively. Her gaze slid round the room. It appeared her honesty hadn't gone down so well with the Sheikha's attendants. "I mean, I'm not worthy…"

"I'm not so sure," Khal's mother argued, waving her attendants forward. "Help this young woman to dress," she commanded.

When Beth was finally turned out to everyone's approval, she spun round to show the Dowager Sheikha, who had seated herself in a chair to watch.

At first there was silence, and then the Dowager Sheikha observed, "You look quite beautiful, my dear, and I hope you enjoy wearing the dress. It belonged to my daughter—"

As the older woman's voice choked off, Beth felt a change in the air. It was as if there was some history behind the Sheikha's comment that everyone but Beth knew about. "Your Majesty," Beth said softly, not wanting to intrude on the Dowager Sheikha's private thoughts. "I'm overwhelmed by your generosity, and I promise to take good care of the dress."

The Sheikha gave her the briefest of nods, and Beth suspected Khal's mother didn't trust herself to speak, because something else had joined them in the room. Grief, Beth thought, wondering at it. "I've taken up enough of your time already," she said to excuse herself. "I'll bring the dress back to you in the morning."

"That won't be necessary," the Sheikha said, tipping her chin in a way that reminded Beth of herself when she tried fighting off uncomfortable memories. "I'll have someone collect it from your apartment after breakfast. And now, if you're ready, my ladies will escort you back to the ballroom."

With the faintest of smiles the Dowager Sheikha signalled that the doors should be opened and everyone should leave her now. She was desperate to be alone with whatever pain had come to join her from the past, Beth sensed.

"You remind me of myself at your age," the Dowager Sheikha murmured as Beth prepared to leave the room. And as Beth made her final curtsey their gazes briefly met and held.

When Beth entered the ballroom this time everyone turned to stare, including His Majesty Khalifa Kadir al Hassan, Sheikh of Sheikhs, the ruler of Q'Adar. And she did feel a little buzz of excitement, Beth admitted to herself. Okay, a roar. But who would have thought it? Here she was, Beth Tracey Torrance, at the royal court in Q'Adar…

Get over it! Beth told herself firmly, *and remember to pick your feet up this time.*

Beth held her head up as a pathway cleared for her across the vast floor. She should enjoy this moment. It wasn't every day you got to wear a fairy-tale gown and parade in front of all these worthies. She walked steadily and then made her way carefully up the steps. She was determined not to fall and ruin the precious dress, which meant no one must be allowed to distract her, not even the man towering over everyone else on the royal dais.

"Ms Torrance…"

Khal's deep, husky voice ran shivers down Beth's spine. It took all she had to blank her mind at where they'd met before, or what she'd seen on that occasion. But that wasn't easy when the scent of his sultry cologne was washing over her, and naughty thoughts were making it hard not to break into nervous giggles.

Making a fool of yourself isn't an option, Beth Tracey Torrance, Beth's inner voice insisted. *Think of your friends back home.* It was true. They were all waiting to hear her news, and she couldn't let them down when any one of them would have loved to be here in her place.

"Your Majesty…" Beth surprised even herself by managing a perfect curtsey, but the only problem with that was that it brought her into close proximity with an area of the Sheikh's body it was far safer not to think about. Thankfully, Khal chose that moment to reach for her hands and raise her to her feet, but when she looked up into his face his expression was grim. What had she done wrong this time?

* * *

His mask almost slipped when he saw the dress his mother had chosen for Beth to wear. Why that dress? Why his sister's dress? Was it because it was the only dress suitable for Beth to wear in his mother's wardrobe? He realised his face was growing increasingly fierce as he fought off emotions he had battled so long to subdue, and he could see the confusion in Beth's eyes. This wasn't her fault, but he couldn't explain to her, not here. Nor could he explain to Beth that when his mother sent her arrows flying her aim was invariably accurate. This was her way of telling him that he had grown cold and unfeeling since the tragedy, and that it was time for him to re-join the world.

He shook himself out of the painful reminiscences, remembering this was Beth's moment, not his. And no one, not even his mother, was going to spoil it for her. Having introduced Beth to the assembled guests, he handed her the trophy. "Congratulations, Ms Torrance," he said formally.

Khal looked so grim, but she had no option but to shake his hand and say thank you. She *had* to. Tilting up her chin, Beth met the gaze of the ruler of Q'Adar, a man who would have been stunningly sexy under any circumstances. But here, with the full weight of his power surrounding him, he was a devastating sight. Yes, except for his lack of emotion he was just about perfect. So why was he so cold? Beth wondered, as Khal stood back, allowing her to take the applause.

It was better for her if he disapproved, she concluded. Did she want him noticing her, smiling at her, wanting her? No, of course not; in fact, she was relieved.

Liar! Beth's inner voice accused her as she turned to face her audience. Still she managed a smile and then thanked everyone politely. "And before you start dancing again…" Silence cloaked the room. She was not supposed to say anything else. Firming her jaw, she continued. "I'd just like to say—" A gasp of astonishment greeted this. Ignoring it, Beth ploughed on, "That this trophy isn't just for me." She waved it in the air. "But for everyone who works at Mr Khadir's stores." Another gasp, much louder than the last. "Yes, I realise you all know him as His Majesty, but to us he's the best boss ever." It was Beth's turn to gasp as someone took firm hold of her elbow. She exclaimed out loud when she realised who it was. "Sorry," she said, but the words just kept on tumbling out. "I bet you can't wait to get rid of me."

"On the contrary," the ruler of Q'Adar murmured in her ear. "I'd just like to save you further embarrassment."

"Well, you don't need to, thank you very much," Beth said, swallowing back her fright as several royal attendants stepped forward to take her into custody. "Do I look like a threat?" she whispered angrily to Khal.

He waved them off. Beth was more of a threat than she knew, Khal thought as he inclined his head towards her in a polite gesture of dismissal. "Enjoy the rest of your evening, Ms Torrance..."

She did, as it happens—enjoy the rest of her evening, that was. She was determined to. She had every intention of delivering a full report on the Platinum and Diamond Ball when she returned home, and no one was going to spoil it for her friends. She was going to keep their dreams intact even if the truth, as she had discovered, was somewhat different. But here at this table it wasn't so hard to find things to report on, because everyone was so nice. Which made a change from the man frowning at her from the royal dais. That was, when Khal could spare a moment from spending time with each of the princesses selected for his attention. Khal's mother would have made a good personal shopper at the store, Beth decided. The Dowager Sheikha had a real knack for bringing tempting selections for the customer to choose from. "How much would one of those cost?" Beth asked her friend Jamilah impishly.

Angling her chin in the direction of Khal and his bevy of princesses, Jamilah hazarded a guess. "Those tiaras probably cost a cool million each, just for starters."

"No, I mean the whole package." Now she had started, Beth couldn't suppress her mischievous Merseyside humour.

"You mean the cost of one princess?" Jamilah said, grinning as she got the joke.

"A country and a camel," someone across their table discreetly offered.

"Ten camels."

"Any advance on ten?"

Their table was now in such uproar that Beth noticed they were attracting disapproving looks. She guessed the young people had never been so outspoken before, and it was all her fault.

"I think we've outstayed our welcome," Jamilah confided in Beth. "We're going back to our family encampment for the fireside celebrations. Would you like to come with us? There'll be dancing."

"Dancing?" Beth couldn't have been more surprised. It made Q'Adar sound like Liverpool, when she was sure the life here for young people couldn't be more different. "Where are you camped?"

"Just outside the palace walls, right on the beach. My relatives will be there and I'm allowed to bring a friend. Everyone's agreed they'd rather have you join us than one of those sacrificial lambs at the royal table." And, when Beth looked askance at her, Jamilah explained. "We all know those girls on the top table have been selected for their beauty, and are only here on approval for the Sheikh to take a look at. His mother can't wait for him to get married and give her grandchildren."

"But that's rather sweet of her, isn't it?" Beth said, not sure quite how she felt about it.

"Not for the sacrificial lambs."

"Point taken," Beth agreed, discreetly slipping away from the table to follow her new-found friends.

"I suggest you get changed out of that dress and leave your trophy in your suite," Jamilah said as they hurried out of the ballroom. "I'll go and find you something suitable to wear, and then I'll come back for you, otherwise you're bound to get lost in the palace—it's such a maze."

Beth's heart lifted as they scurried along the grand, vaulted corridor as fast as their high heels would allow. It looked as if she was going to have something good to tell her friends about after all.

He watched her leave, and knew where she'd be heading when he saw who had befriended her. He was pleased for Beth. He was glad she had found some companions of her own age to make her stay a happy one until she left Q'Adar. And it would be a wonderful experience for her to mix with his people without all this pomp and ceremony getting in the way.

No. He wasn't pleased, Khal decided, frowning. Jamilah's male relatives would be present, along with every other hot-blooded man in the palace who had been invited to take part in the open-air celebrations. Chaperoned or not, there would be opportunities for the sexes to mix, and Beth was impressionable.

He stood. It was a signal for everyone else in the grand ballroom to stand too. He gestured that they must all sit down again, and then he used the microphone to wish them an enjoyable evening. An evening he would no longer be part of. He ignored his mother's scandalised glances as he left the dais. The Sheikh of Sheikhs wasn't required to give a reason when he decided the entertainment on offer no longer held sufficient appeal. He had done his duty by the princesses, having reviewed the parade of hopefuls, and now those painted dolls could return home and take their greedy black eyes with them. He'd made enough deals in his life to know when he was being duped.

Back in her glamorous palace accommodation Beth was excited. It was good to finally be part of something where she was welcome—not that she had ever envisioned being drawn into the royal circle, of course. The Dowager Sheikha had been extremely kind to lend her the dress, Beth thought as she carefully hung it up on a padded hanger. Then she went red, remembering her speech, and Khal dragging her away from the microphone. How had she dared to speak out like that?

She had dared, and it hadn't been all that bad, Beth thought, sharing a twinkle with her reflection. Maybe what this country needed was some down-to-earth action. There was far too much la-di-dah bowing and scraping going on, from what she'd seen. And she was pretty sure Khal wasn't comfortable with it either.

When had she started thinking of him as "Khal"? Beth wondered. On the beach, she realised—when he'd been naked with nothing but a towel to cover his country's assets! And now she must try not to think about him at all. About how hot he'd looked in his simple Bedouin robes... They had clung to his body as he'd strode purposefully about, prompting all sorts of wicked thoughts. If she ever saw him in a pair of snug-fitting jeans she'd probably faint clean away! But as sheikhs didn't wear jeans she was safe, Beth concluded with relief as she showered down under tepid water. Having brushed her hair, she wrapped a robe round herself and waited with suppressed excitement for Jamilah to come back for her.

A few minutes later Beth stared at the outfit Jamilah was holding out to her. "Oh, but I couldn't possibly..."

"You don't like it?" Jamilah's face fell.

"Oh no," Beth quickly explained. "I mean, it's so beautiful I couldn't possibly wear it."

"Unless I insist, and assure you I'll be deeply offended if you don't?"

As both girls laughed companionably, Jamilah helped Beth dress, arranging the floating chiffon of the Arabian gown to best advantage. In subtle shades of powder blue and silver, the yards of fabric took a lot of taming. "I'd never have managed it on my own," Beth admitted, staring at herself in amazement in the mirror. "Would you take a picture of me?" she said, thinking of her friends as she snatched up the camera.

"Of course I will. You look really beautiful."

"I certainly look different, but it's your beautiful dress that makes the difference," Beth argued in her usual down-to-earth way.

"Just one final touch," Jamilah told her, draping a panel of the flimsy headdress across Beth's face.

Beth's eyes widened as they approached the encampment. She had never seen anything like it in her life. With the fire blazing high into the sky in front of the ocean, and the musicians beating their Arabian drums and strumming even more exotic instruments, it was like the setting for a film. Jamilah's family tents were vast and decked out with pennants and gold hangings, with the symbol of a hawk prominently displayed next to something written in Arabic script.

"Khalifa," Jamilah said, noticing Beth was looking at it. "Though it's a reference to my family's loyalty to the Sheikh of Sheikhs, and there are no designer shoes other than mine in our tent, unfortunately."

Beth laughed at the reference to the Khalifa luxury brand. Would she ever get used to this mix of East and West? It couldn't have been more starkly illustrated. But as the warm breeze caressed her face she forgot the comparisons. "It's so beautiful here," she breathed, moving closer to the ocean on sandaled feet. The night breeze was making the ruby satin curtains outside the tents dance, and the susurration of the waves breaking on the shore was so soothing she barely noticed Jamilah slipping away and someone else taking her place.

He could move freely in the dark, and as yet his face was not widely recognised. His title meant nothing now, and the usual restrictions did not exist here in this temporary tented city outside the palace walls. He headed away from the music, following silently in the footsteps Beth was leaving on the sand. He waited as she slipped off her sandals, admiring the way she looked in traditional dress. She wore it well, with all the grace of a true Q'Adaran, and he could tell she was enchanted by the romance of wearing the flowing robes of an Arabian princess. She didn't even know Jamilah was his cousin, or that Q'Adaran women could be as subtle in their matchmaking endeavours as their Western counterparts. And for once he was grateful to the mischievous Jamilah, for no one but she knew he was there.

Khal in snug-fitting jeans? No, she must be dreaming.

"Khal?" Beth swallowed hard, rooted to the spot as the music started up again and drowned out her voice. What should she do now? Should she carry on walking out along the beach, or... It didn't matter what she did, Beth's sensible self insisted, since the Sheikh of Sheikhs could hardly be here to seek out her company. But as Khal blocked her way Beth realised she was wrong.

"You shouldn't be walking along the beach on your own."

"Jamilah told me I'd be safe here."

"There are so many people..." Khal gazed out across the tented city, while Beth's throat tightened to the point where she doubted she could speak at all.

"Do you dance?" he said, turning to her.

"Do I dance?" Beth repeated foolishly wondering if that really was a touch of humour tugging at the corner of Khal's mouth. And in his eyes... The dance was already inside her, she realised, and it was both an erotic and an irresistible temptation. "Of course I dance," she said. "Don't you?"

This time he really smiled; there was no doubt about it. "Shall we?" he said, offering her his hand.

Where had that attractive crease in his cheek come from? "Do you mean you want to dance with me?" Beth gazed at Khal's outstretched hand.

"That's the general idea."

Beth Tracey Torrance dances with the Sheikh on the beach! No toes broken—thanks to being barefoot! That would be her headline. But did she trust herself to hold Khal's hand?

Khal took the decision for Beth, drawing her to him and yet holding her at arm's length so that they were barely touching. But it wasn't enough to make her resist the seductive rhythms of the Q'Adaran music. "Do you come here often?" Beth whispered cheekily, still wanting to pinch herself in case this was a dream.

"Never quite like this," Khal admitted, playing along. "But that could change."

"What would it take to change, Your Majesty?" Beth glanced shyly up.

"Khal," he murmured, holding her gaze until Beth thought she might never breathe again. And his smile was back. *Please let it last this time*, she silently begged. She didn't want him to change; she wanted this moment to last for ever.

When the music stopped they stood together in silence, and when it started up again in a much slower rhythm His Majesty Khalifa Kadir al Hassan, Sheikh of Sheikhs, Bringer of Light to His People drew her so close she could feel his heart beating against her breasts. Her nipples grew instantly taut at the subtle stimulation. Surely he must feel the change in them? There was no doubt in her mind that Beth Tracey Torrance had turned into a wanton hussy.

A wanton hussy with precious little common sense, Beth told herself impatiently, pulling away.

As Khal pulled her back again Beth knew she was on the point of stepping over a boundary from which there would be no turning back. So she must resist. Of course she must resist! But the lure of her surroundings combined with her need to feel wanted made it hard—no, impossible—

to resist. And so she rested against Khal's hard, warm body, knowing the strength to pull away had completely deserted her. She was on fire for him, and could feel every inch of him pressed up hard against her, while streams of sensation went pulsing through her veins...

The report to her friends would have to end here, Beth decided as Khal's hand settled in the hollow at the small of her back. With his fingers splayed across the top of her buttocks, and her body pounding with desire, the rest of the night would be X-rated, and as such it would have to be censored.

CHAPTER FIVE

SEX With A Sheikh was a cocktail, not an option, Beth reminded herself as Khal took hold of her hand and drew her with him. As the lights of the campfire faded behind them, and the laughter and conversation subsided beneath the rush of the surf, she was cloaked in awareness as he stopped walking and brought her to face him.

Was this was really happening, or should she pinch herself? Her hand felt so safe in his, as he drew her inch by inch towards him, she didn't even pretend to resist. Beneath a rich blue velvet sky studded with diamonds, this was so magical her throat had closed with emotion. Things like this didn't happen to her; no one had ever treated her as if she was precious and fragile before. Khal could take his pick from any number of women, but he had chosen her. Closing her eyes, she inhaled his cologne. It was the most wonderful fragrance, but more intoxicating still was the man holding her. And, when she finally allowed her muscles to soften against him, Beth knew she was more aroused than she had ever been, and that was dangerous.

How long had it been since he'd held a woman like this? Had he ever held a woman like this?— as if she might break? By this stage he would expect any play mate to be pressing themselves against him as though they were on heat, telling him without words what he could take and what it would cost him. But not Beth.

Beth…

He should pull back now. He should recognise the way he felt about her for the warning it was and pull back now. But as he took a step back she reached out to him. He looked at her outstretched hand. It was so tiny, she was so tiny. What he should do now was throw her a careless smile and tell her he'd enjoyed the dance, before sending her back to the encampment and Jamilah, where she'd be safe. "Shall we walk a while?" he said instead.

"Okay, if that's what you want," she said lightly. Her chin lifted as she spoke, and a rogue breeze tossed her hair across her face. As he reached out to remove the strands from her lips, she moved too and their hands caught and tangled. Instead of snatching hers away, she let it rest in his and held his gaze. The fact that she trusted him enough to do that resonated strongly with him. And so he pulled away. She was young, and he must bring this to an end now.

She saw the change in his eyes right away. "What's wrong, Khal?"

He said nothing, but she felt him distancing himself from her.

"Am I such a threat to you? To Q'Adar?"

"Don't be ridiculous."

"No, I'm not being ridiculous. You're pushing me away."

And with that she picked up the skirts of her eastern dress and ran away from him down the beach, with her sandals in her hand. That should have set the seal on his determination to let her go, but instead it just etched a deeper groove in his mind for her to occupy, and so he went after her.

Beth quailed when she heard Khal coming after her. Her chest was burning and her legs had turned to jelly. There were so many feelings exploding inside her, she was confused. She wanted a moment—and there was no time. He was here. He was right here behind her.

"Beth…"

His voice called softly, but the call reached deep inside her and made her turn. "Khal…" She had the rest of her life to find out who she was, the rest of her life to be Beth Tracey Torrance with no one's expectation weighing on her shoulders. Couldn't she spare a moment for him, a moment for His Majesty, just to say goodbye and thank him for his hospitality?

Beth uncurled her fists, releasing the tension in her fingers. She wouldn't run from him. Maybe Khal needed a moment to talk to an ordinary person.

She looked so adorable, and even more beautiful than usual in the floating gown. But it was more than her innocence and beauty that captivated him. Beth had made him see things he hadn't noticed before, she made him think a different way; she made him question everything he had always believed in. As he stood in front of her he leaned forward, meaning to brush her cheek with his lips, but then she took a step towards him and turned her face up so he brushed her mouth instead.

Her eyes closed, but she didn't move or speak, and then the warm breeze gave them its blessing, bringing her another step closer, until all thoughts of resisting the temptation of kissing Beth had fled from his mind. She tasted sweet and warm, and the scent of wildflowers rose from her hair, invading his senses until he could no longer think. He barely touched her; she seemed so fragile, so tiny. It was a whisper of a kiss, or at least that was how it started. But Beth was innocently demanding, surprising him with the depths of her passion, a passion he guessed was new to her and that she had no idea how to curb. It made her bolder than he had anticipated, as well as sweeter and more fragile, and as she wrapped her arms around his neck, clinging on tight to tell him fiercely that she needed him as much as he needed her, he wanted so badly to believe it was true. As Beth's words poured into his soul, his world expanded with possibility. It was as if they knew each other already, and had merely been separated for a while. How easy it would be to pick up where they had left off… If he could just switch off his conscience.

But it had already kicked in, reminding him of all the things that stood between them—duty, honour and Beth's innocence, the barrier he would never cross. And so on the very point of deepening the kiss he drew back.

"Why did you do that?" she said.

"I apologise," he said formally. "I forgot myself."

"You forgot how to kiss?" Her eyes were sparkling; even now she couldn't help the humour. Plus there was some unfathomable bond between them that, incongruous and unlikely though it might be, refused to break.

"Are you saying I'm too much for you, Khal?" she teased him gently.

Her brand of innocent humour made him smile. Too much for him? She was sensational. Naïve? Yes. She was also tiny, blonde and vulnerable—but it was her inner fire that warmed him through. But that was not his fire to take comfort by, it was for some other man in Beth's future, a man who could offer her all the things she deserved. "How old are you?" he said, meaning it as a gentle rebuke.

"Old enough," she assured him cheekily in a way that told him she knew nothing of the effect those words could have on a man.

"That's a dangerous thing to say, Beth Tracey Torrance."

"But not to you," she said, with trust that touched him deeply. "And anyway," she said. "I've done with safe." She paused to brush the hair out of her eyes as the wind tossed it about. "And I wouldn't be here in Q'Adar if I'd wanted boring, would I?"

He recognised the voice of innocence speaking, and, stamping down on his desires, he made no reply.

"It's that duty of yours again, isn't it?" she said. "Not that I'm criticising you—far from it." Mashing her lips together as she thought about it, she said bluntly, "I think you're wonderful. And I think the people of Q'Adar are lucky to have you. I trust you, which is why I know your people can trust you. You put duty above everything, and that's what makes you so special..." Breaking off, she started to frown again. "But it must be a burden sometimes, mustn't it?"

He tensed as her frown turned to compassion. Beth's incessant questioning challenged him at every opportunity, and in that they were the same. When did he not question the status quo? Yet at the same time Beth and he were so far apart. "Duty?" He gave her a wry smile. "Duty is never a burden, Beth. You can't always have everything you want in life."

"And *you* can never have it." she protested, "Because your fate is tied in to your kingdom."

"Exactly."

"Well, I'm going to have it all," she said passionately.

"You are?" He felt a stirring of unease. Would she disappoint him now?

"Yes!" she exclaimed. "I'm going to have kids, family, love, job, happiness—everything!"

Her eyes blazed with such certainty, it was a lesson in just how wrong he'd been to doubt her. She hadn't worked out the finer details yet, but nothing daunted her. Disappoint him? She had only increased his passion for her tenfold, plus he envied her, he admired her, and most of all he wanted her. He wanted for just a moment to share in Beth's freedom, and in her belief in a future full of so many wonderful things.

The look she gave him now turned the heat inside him into a raging inferno, and when he dragged her close this time he had no intention of letting go. He felt her legs give way as he swung her into his arms, and knew as he did so that he had never felt like this before, and that he never would again.

So this was what it felt like to be held as if you mattered to someone. And even if it was only for one night she was going to treasure every single second of it. Khal rounded the point to his own private beach where he told her they wouldn't be disturbed. Not even his security forces were allowed to trespass here, though there were men patrolling the perimeter. He carried her into the cool of the shadows beneath the rocks, and, dropping his towel, spread it out for them on the sand. Lowering her gently, he lay down at her side and kissed her again.

Khal kissed her deeply, teasing her lips apart with his tongue, and that together with the heat and taste of him drew a moan of approval from somewhere deep inside her. This was a dream, it had to be. How else could she play with fire and feel so safe?

As she reached up to cup his face, Khal took her hands and laced their fingers together in a gesture of closeness and trust that made her heart squeeze tight. Then he drew back, and, resting on one elbow, stared into her eyes. She had a feeling of being small, of being no one, while she was lying here with a man who occupied such a huge space on the world stage.

"Don't look so anxious," Khal murmured, kissing her so amazingly she was quickly reassured.

He stroked her with the lightest of touches, enjoying the sight of her quivering with desire. He shivered too, internally, as restraint took its toll. But as her eyes drifted shut and she murmured his name he cupped her face in his hands and kissed her...

"Kiss me again," she whispered the moment he released her. She had no idea how she was torturing him or she wouldn't wind her arms around his neck like this, breathing his name so it sounded like a feather on a breath of wind, a feather that had the power to travel to his heart and pierce it like an arrow.

She pulled him back when he pulled away. "Don't leave me," she begged him in a way that pierced his heart a second time. But when he kissed her now, and felt her shudder of desire through every part of him, he knew it would soon be beyond his mortal powers to hold back. He tried hushing and soothing her, as he might have calmed a restless colt, but trying to hold Beth back while she in her innocence was trying to hurry him on only upped the level of torture for them both.

"Khal, I know I'm not what you need…"

As she began to excuse and explain how she felt he was so incredulous, so defensive on her behalf, that all he could think was that Beth was exactly what he needed. And so why was he holding back? With all the riches of Q'Adar at his disposal, he felt blessed that fate had brought her to him. "You're special," he told her. "And don't you ever forget that, Beth Tracey Torrance." He was staring deep into her eyes, into her soul, when she answered him with perfect logic.

"Then, if you don't care who I am, what's

standing between us? Because there is some-thing, isn't there?"

"Yes," he admitted. "My concern for you. I care about you, Beth. I care about you very much in-deed."

She thought about this for a moment, her face serious and intent, and he saw then that beneath all Beth's light-hearted talk she was a deep thinker who, even now after so short an acquain-tance, longed for something he could never give her—a family and exclusivity. How could he do that when the very thought of it was out of his reach? And even had they known each other lon-ger he was married to his country. They both knew that whatever happened between them now was for today, and only for today, because his life and all he was belonged to Q'Adar.

The thrust of Khal's tongue was so bold Beth felt a wild urge to tear off her clothes and offer her breasts for his approval. Her innocence pre-vented her doing more than imagining how that might feel, but she was aching for him so badly in secret places she hardly dared to think what it would be like to have him touch her intimately...

Some force must have taken her over, Beth reasoned. This force, as elemental as the sea and as powerful as the man lying next to her took no account that she was inexperienced. It was a power that acknowledged no master, and only one goal...

The erotic daydream came to an abrupt end. Could Khal have changed his mind? Beth wondered as he sat up suddenly. "There isn't room for both of us on the towel..." Uncertain of her ground, she tried to make it sound like a question.

Khal didn't reply at once, and instead brushed the sand from his thighs—which drew her attention to his powerful legs, legs she could so easily imagine wrapped around her. And then he firmed his lips as if he had made his decision.

"Don't..." She didn't want to hear whatever it was he had to say. She couldn't bear to hear him say he didn't want her. "Don't stop now," she murmured self-consciously, closing her eyes against the expression on his face. "Or I shall think you don't want me."

Khal's answer was to sweep her into his arms so she could feel every inch of him intimately. His energy surrounded her, softening her, empowering her... This felt so right, and yet Khal must have sensed some small remaining doubt inside her and, instead of growing more passionate, he eased her down onto the ground at his side. "Beth, if this is all too fast for you..."

"No." She breathed the word short and fast, closing her eyes, willing him not to pull away. She couldn't bear anything to come between them—not his duty, and certainly not her fear. If this was all they had, this short time together, then she embraced it wholeheartedly. "Kiss me..." *Kiss away my fears*, she begged silently, rejoicing when she felt Khal's warm breath brush her face.

As the shadows gave way to the moon they matched their strength against each other. Khal was always careful, always tender, so that Beth's trust in him could only grow. She in turn grew bolder and more confident, learning to laugh and to relax in his arms. She enjoyed the simple pleasure of being close to him, and for now she wanted nothing more. She clutched his chest and rubbed her face against his naked skin. She loved the sure touch of his hands on her, and the hot words he was whispering to her in a language she didn't understand. She even found the courage to loosen the waistband of her chiffon skirt when the fabric became twisted round her legs. And when she arched her back this time Khal's hands slipped down to cup her buttocks, and she whispered, "Yes..." Smiling against his lips, she repeated, "Oh yes..."

Beth's spirit and her growing confidence made him smile, made him realise there was a lot more to his feelings for her than he had first thought. While he was examining them, she tugged off the rest of her clothes. "Tease," he accused her softly, filled with happiness because she was so happy. She was so impulsive, full of life and mischief. She lifted the weight from his shoulders and made him feel young again. And how could he fail to notice that without a bra her breasts were magnificent? His first impulse was to lose himself in them, but again he drew back.

"What's wrong now?" she said, proudly displaying them.

She was so beautiful, and had no idea of the power under her command. He wanted her to discover the mystical powers a woman possessed slowly and completely. But Beth was so inquisitive and fearless. He was many things, but not a saint, and as her tiny hands closed around him, stroking insistently and persuasively, he hardened into steel.

She was fast losing focus. She couldn't hide her hunger for stimulation and release much longer, but Khal was more experienced than she knew, and he couldn't be led. He would set his own pace, Beth realised when she tried to guide him. "What must I do?" she whimpered, half to herself. She could see him smiling.

"Be patient."

"What do you mean?"

"Lie back and you'll find out. Look at me," Khal instructed her softly when she finally relaxed back on the ground. "And lie still..."

How was she supposed to relax and lie still while he was slipping one powerful thigh between her legs? She couldn't stop moving when she was so excited and aroused, but as Khal feathered strokes down her body she slipped into a delicious lethargy, and lay still to enjoy each spine-tingling sensation. He broke her trance by hooking his fingertips beneath her lacy briefs, to which she responded by wriggling furiously to help him get them down.

"Lie still; I thought I told you," he murmured, smiling against her lips.

Still? Was he crazy? She had never felt so sensitive and aware before. Every single part of her was wired for pleasure, and with every ragged breath she took she was moving closer to desperation.

"Don't rush me," Khal insisted wickedly against her lips.

She was telling him about tender, throbbing places waiting to be pleasured, but he wasn't going to rush, he had every intention of savouring this. Seeing her naked beneath him, palest gold against his bronze, made him want to do more than have sex with her. He wanted to taste, stroke, and watch Beth's eyes darken with pleasure when she pressed her cushioned softness against him. The sight of her made him greedy, but for the sake of her innocence he would wait.

Beth wondered at her emotions. This was all so new and dangerous to her, and the feelings inside her had far more to do with love than mere physical pleasure—and that was scary. "I love it when you kiss me," she told Khal softly. She was experiencing feelings so new and tender she couldn't bring herself to speak them out loud— and so instead she reached for him, arching her back and aching for release, longing for reassurance, and needing more commitment than she was sure the ruler of Q'Adar could give.

CHAPTER SIX

As Beth arched her back, resting her hands above her head in an attitude of innocent sensuality, Khal found the urge to bring her pleasure overwhelming. But still he held back, knowing delay would bring its own rewards. He gave her lingering kisses on her lips and on her neck. He suckled her nipples until she writhed helplessly beneath him, begging for more. He lavished his attention on her soft, warm belly, and was impatient to discover if this cushioned perfection extended to every part of her.

While they were kissing he removed his shirt, and the sensation of naked flesh on flesh hit him like an electric shock. The one thing he hadn't bargained for was Beth releasing the fastening on his jeans while he was recovering. It made him laugh at her audacity, it made him hold her in his arms and transmit all that he was feeling into her eyes. It felt so right, so good to him, and as they wrestled playfully he discovered they fit together perfectly, even though he was so much bigger than she was. She was like a tiny, tender kernel at the heart of a ripe fruit and as she strained towards him, drawing her legs back in anticipation of even more pleasure, he teased her with the tip. Almost at once the pleasure waves threatened, and as she bucked towards him, exclaiming in excitement, he drew back. "Not yet..."

"Why not?" she demanded, eyes wide as she struggled to understand the complexities of lovemaking.

"Because I enjoy teasing you."

"Then I'll have to take matters into my own hands," she threatened, though he knew she would wait for him to set the pace. Escaping her grasp, he moved down, tasting and teasing her, preparing her and laving her with his tongue until she rolled her head from side to side, gasping with excitement. There was no awkwardness between them now, just hot, hungry need, and as he eased her legs apart even more she gripped his shoulders and stared into his eyes, showing him how much she trusted him. Pouting, silky warmth greeted him, a playground in which to lose himself, a welcoming cushion where he could sink.

"Now," she begged him. "Now!" she cried out more insistently. "I want more of you... I want all of you..."

He sank into her like coming home, wondering if he had the willpower to endure such pleasure. Beth's fingers bit into his shoulders while he moved carefully at first, and then firmly and rhythmically to give her the satisfaction she craved. He plunged deep and then withdrew, so that it was like taking her for the first time over and over again, and she cried out with increasing pleasure at each stroke. He was sorry when it was over for her too soon, and realised it was a measure of her inexperience, but as she cried out his name he used all his wiles to prolong the pleasure for her. He wanted her to enjoy every moment. And when she quietened he continued to move gently and insistently, kissing her all the while until he felt her respond.

"You're amazing," she whispered, starting to work her hips against him. How could she be ready for more? But she was. Incredibly, she was. He had awoken something in Beth that matched his own hunger, and it touched him to see her blossoming into a woman in his arms.

Khal never tired. How could that be? He was at her service, pleasuring her until she couldn't stop herself, and until all thoughts of control had vanished from her mind. She was greedy for him, and he was offering her a feast. When he withdrew briefly one time she weighed him in her hands, marvelling at his size, and wondering at the pleasure he could give her. She was on the point of asking him directly where his stamina came from when he moved behind her, bringing his leg over hers, and trapping her in the most deliciously receptive position imaginable, telling her, "I think you'll enjoy the Q'Adaran way now…"

"I'm sure I will," she agreed, gasping a little when Khal pressed her forward and took her again. He moved so deeply he stretched her, and, at the same time as setting up a regular rhythm, the hand that wasn't pressing her forward was playing a delicate game with fingertips that brought such extremes of pleasure she could only moan her appreciation in time to each stroke and thrust.

"Yes?" Khal husked against her back.

Did he expect her to speak? She could only make a sound like an animal urging him on. How many times was it now? So many times. And this time was so powerful she must have passed out for a moment—because the next thing she knew she was safely nestled in Khal's arms, and he was stroking her and kissing her, lulling her to sleep.

"Can't we stay here for ever?" Beth asked Khal later, impulsively, when they emerged hand in hand from the sea. They had made love again beneath the stars and the moon, and with the ocean bathing their limbs in warm, limpid water.

"For ever is a long time."

His words sent a shiver down her back. Only minutes before she had been resting on a pillow of undulating water with her legs locked round Khal's waist. His feet had been firmly planted on the sea bed, while she gazed at the stars and dreamed of "for ever". Now it seemed her cries of release had mingled with the surf and carried those dreams away. She had spoken carelessly. It sounded foolish and childish to her now, and as Khal let go of her hand Beth felt he must think so too. Returning to dry land was a return to reality for both of them. The sheikh and the shop girl's relative positions in life had been firmly re-established. Making love with Khal had been the most extraordinary experience of her life, as well as the most deeply moving…for her. *But for him*… Was it over now?

"I'll take you back when you're dressed," Khal said.

"I'd like to go straight back to my room, if you don't mind?" Beth said, proud of herself when her voice remained as steady as his. She still had her pride. "I need to shower all this salt off me."

"Of course."

Khal's matter-of-fact tone spoke more clearly than any words could about the wedge between them, and it was growing wider all the time. The fairy-tale was over, Beth thought, casting a wistful glance behind them at the ocean.

The clock struck as they arrived back in the courtyard outside Beth's room. Was it possible she had only been with Khal so short a time? It had felt like a lifetime of growing closer and learning to trust, until the doubt had set in. Beth paused with her hand resting on the rough stone archway, watching Khal stride away. He was purposeful now, moving on to the next part of his life. They had parted with the briefest of caresses—just a touch of his hand on her face. If she closed her eyes she could still feel it...

"Ms Torrance."

Beth gasped guiltily and swung around to see the Dowager Sheikha approaching. "I'm sorry, Your Majesty, have you been looking for me?"

The Dowager Sheikha took a step back, and her gaze swept over Beth. "I missed you in the ballroom. They told me you had left the palace, and I wanted to be sure you were safe. I want you to leave Q'Adar with happy memories. You have enjoyed your stay, Ms Torrance?"

"Oh, yes, Your Majesty!" Beth exclaimed, her honesty bursting through the need for caution. Beth blushed deep red, realising she had almost betrayed herself. Had the Dowager Sheikha seen her son leave the courtyard?

"You're a sweet child, and I can tell that my son is very much taken with you."

"Oh?" Beth bit down on her lip, acutely conscious of how tender and swollen it was after all

Khal's kisses, and she knew that her cheeks must still be red from the rasp of his stubble.

"You don't have to pretend with me, Ms Torrance. Hard as it may be for you to believe, I was young once, and I too met a sheikh under unusual circumstances…"

Beth wished she could think of something to say to allay the Dowager Sheikha's fears. Having seen the beautiful princesses, she knew Khal's mother had high hopes for her son's marriage. But what could she say? It wasn't her way to lie or fudge an issue, and she could hardly confess the truth. *The truth*. The *truth* was burning its way through her heart. She dipped into another curtsey. "I'm sorry if I disturbed you, Your Majesty, it's very late, and I'm sure you must be tired."

"Time means nothing here in Q'Adar, Ms Torrance. It is measured in millennia, rather than hours or minutes, and if you come with me now I would like to show you something that will open your eyes to the scale of things here in my country."

Beth wondered what the Dowager Sheikha could possibly mean as she followed her across the courtyard. She climbed behind her, up the steep stone steps leading to the ramparts, where they could see for miles over the surrounding desert. Beth gasped as she took it all in. As far as the eyes could see campfires lit the darkness. She hadn't realised how far the tented city extended when she had been down on the beach. "There must be thousands of people down there," she breathed.

"Hundreds of thousands," Khal's mother confirmed, turning to face her. "Now do you understand the weight my son carries? Do you see now why he is wedded to duty? These people have come from all over His Majesty's kingdom to greet him on his birthday. They have come to swear their loyalty to him, Beth. May I call you Beth? And thousands more will be here by tomorrow, all wanting to bask in the strength and the hope that is His Majesty Khalifa Kadir al Hassan, Sheikh of Sheikhs, Bringer of Light to His People. They believe in him, Beth. Look at them…" The Dowager Sheikha's gesture encompassed the whole desert encampment. "All these people rely on my son to lead them out of darkness and poverty into a new, brighter future.

Would you have him distracted from the path of duty? Would you take him from Q'Adar?"

"I would never do that!" Beth exclaimed.

"Not intentionally, perhaps. But because I loved his father so deeply I know when love is all-consuming, and when there is no space in your heart for anything else. My son loves Q'Adar, and that is how it must remain."

"There's no need for you to worry."

"There is every need," the Dowager Sheikha insisted. "I have seen the way you look at my son, and I have seen the way he looks at you."

"But we hardly know each other…" Beth bit her lip, hating the lie, hating every second of this deception.

"How long does it take to fall in love, Beth? Is there a prescribed time?"

"Of course not, but—"

"I ask you again," Khal's mother said gently, turning her face into the wind so she could stare out across the tented city. "Would you take my son from his people?"

"Of course not. I would never take something that didn't belong to me." But her voice had started shaking, betraying emotions Beth hadn't even admitted to herself. She wasn't prepared for this, how could she be? "I do like—the Sheikh," she admitted haltingly. She loved Khal more than life itself, Beth realised now. It had happened in an instant, the moment she'd first laid eyes on him. "But I know who he is, and I know who I am."

"And I think you underestimate both yourself and my son, Beth."

"So what do you want me to do? I'm leaving tomorrow."

"And if he should try to stop you?"

The possibility that Khal might do that was so far from Beth's thinking she couldn't even answer.

"You're a good girl," his mother told her, patting Beth's cheek. "And I think you are standing here with me now with only the very best of intentions in your heart."

"Oh, I am," Beth insisted, wishing she could think of something to say to reassure Khal's mother.

"Forgive an old lady her concerns, but since the death of his sister, Ghayda, Khal is my only child..."

As the Dowager Sheikha's features crumpled into grief, Beth realised this was why she'd sensed some deep-rooted sadness in both Khal and his mother. She remained silent, allowing the woman to talk, and wishing she could think of something to say to Khal's mother that might help.

"Since Ghayda's death, my son has been like ice. I have seen him come to life in the past few hours, because you have my beloved Ghayda's warmth and spirit, and Khal sees this. He believes himself responsible for his sister's death, Beth, and nothing I can say to him will change his mind. But they were both so young and beautiful at the time of the tragedy, both so reckless and irresponsible. They both knew the dangers of the desert, and they were both equally to blame," the Dowager Sheikha said with finality. With a ragged sigh, she turned towards the steps.

Beth followed, wondering why Khal's mother had chosen to trust her with this precious revelation. It was almost as if the she was giving her the seal of approval. And, after hearing it, all Beth wanted to do was rush to Khal and put her arms around him so she could hold him close until the pain went away.

She had to hold on to reality, Beth told herself, and remember that what had happened on the beach with Khal was one isolated incident. It might have been life-changing for her—she would remember that first time for ever—but for Khal it had meant nothing, and she could hardly expect to see him again after tonight. So, whatever secret hopes his mother might be harbouring, they were just daydreams like her own wistful thoughts. "You're very kind, Your Majesty, and I wish I could say something that could express my sadness for your loss."

"Your being here and allowing me to talk to you like this is the kindness," the older woman assured her. Reaching out, she touched Beth's face. "*Ma'salama*, Beth Torrance. Go in peace, my child..."

CHAPTER SEVEN

MONTHS had passed since she had left Q'Adar, and yet here she was, still struggling to accept the freezing rain falling day after day in the north of England. The sunshine in Q'Adar seemed a million miles away, and her time with Khal a distant dream. Dipping her head into the wind, Beth pulled up the collar on her coat, and walked as fast as she could towards the store. It threatened to be a busy morning, what with the planning meeting for the Christmas window-display. She was representing her department at the annual meeting for the first time this year, and had been up at dawn polishing her ideas.

Beth stopped abruptly as she turned the final corner, everything inside her twisting as she stared foolishly at the low-slung limousine with its blacked-out windows. Who else travelled with outriders and merited their own special-force-officers clutching guns? Beth held tight to the latest selection of magazines she'd brought to scan in her lunch hour a little closer. Since Khal's spectacular party, the press had been rife with speculation about when the most eligible bachelor in the Arab world would get married. The gossip about him had even overshadowed the uprising in Q'Adar. You could hardly open a magazine without seeing a picture of Khal blazing from it. The whole world including Beth knew that the ruler of Q'Adar must take a bride—the only questions were who, and when…?

Well, it wouldn't be a Liverpool shop-girl, would it? Beth told herself, starting forward again. And this Liverpool shop girl had a job to do. Tipping her chin at a determined angle, Beth walked briskly towards the staff entrance. The doorman welcomed her with his usual banter, and when he made some comment about their visitor Beth replied calmly, "Ah, well, we all knew we were due a visit one day, didn't we? I missed him last time he was in Liverpool."

"But you must have met him in Q'Adar?"

She was always bright and breezy, but today she didn't want to stop and chat. All she could think was: *Khal's here?* But she had to say something, because everyone and his wife knew she'd been to Q'Adar and had met the Sheikh. "Briefly," Beth agreed, hating the lie as she turned for the lift. "I met him briefly." She stared up at the floor numbers on the panel above the sleek steel doors, wishing the lift would come quickly so the doorman couldn't see her cheeks were on fire.

She survived walking into the boardroom and having the Managing Director introduce each of them in turn. She survived the all-pervading, and oh, so familiar scent of him: wealth, sandalwood, and warm, clean man. She even survived the sight of Khal in a dark bespoke suit that skimmed every inch of his powerful frame, enhancing it almost more than his Arabian robes. She even managed to keep her cool when Khal chose to sit in the centre of his team directly opposite her. She survived all that. But Beth wasn't sure she could endure Khal's penetrating stare for very much longer.

"Ms Torrance?" he invited, in a voice that warmed every part of her, a voice that was entirely professional and emotion-free. "Would you like to give us your suggestions now?"

She had a few for him, Beth thought, feeling hurt rise up inside her. How could Khal have just walked away after everything that had happened between them? And she didn't just mean the sex—they'd drawn closer and seen inside each other's minds; they'd made love. Well, she had. And he hadn't even said goodbye to her before she'd left the country.

What was the point in going over everything in the past? This was the present, this was business; this was real life, and not a fantasy of her own making in Q'Adar.

Khal had taken over the room with the sheer weight of his presence, and as he sat forward attentively Beth knew she had to be as professional about this meeting as he was. She was good at presentations when she believed in something, and she was here to represent her team. She had no intention of letting them down.

He had invented the flimsiest of reasons to be at a meeting he knew she would attend. No one had questioned him; no one had dared. He had taken over the Managing Director's office for the day, and now he was forced to sit here as if he had nothing more on his mind than the Christmas window-displays at Khalifa, when the truth was he wanted Beth. He had tried and failed to put her out of his mind, and so he had come for her.

But as the meeting progressed he found himself drawn in and captivated all over again. He had always thought Beth younger than her years, but in this formal business setting he was seeing another side of her. He could understand why she excelled at her job now. This presentation was thorough, disciplined and innovative. Beth had researched her subject well, and had the statistics to hand to prove her case, as well as an impressive line in persuasion. She would get the budget she requested; favouritism didn't come into it. Where was the need, when Beth's proposal succeeded on two fronts: originality and sound business-sense?

"You've got it," he said, refocusing when she displayed her final budget calculations. She looked at him then for the first time, straight in the eyes.

"I have?" She flushed, unable to hide how thrilled she was. For him that was pure Beth.

His senses stirred as he realised when he'd last seen that sort of colour on her face.

The meeting concluded without any suspicions being aroused as to why the owner of the Khalifa brand had decided to make a surprise visit, and later Beth brought her portfolio of ideas to the office he was borrowing as he'd asked her to. The secretary had already left for lunch, and so it fell to him to take them from her. "You can leave them with me…" For her sake he had meant to keep it brief, but he had forgotten how she affected him. She walked past him and went to stand in the furthest corner of the room, with her back turned to him.

"How could you do that to me?" she said, without turning.

"Walk away?" he said, thinking back to Q'Adar. "I needed time to think. We both did."

"I don't mean in Q'Adar. I mean just now in the boardroom." Slowly, she turned. "First you arrive without warning anyone, and then—" She stopped, clearly fighting back emotion.

"And then?" he prompted gently.

"Why did you look at me like that?" she asked him in a small voice.

"I thought I was being extremely professional."

She shook her head. "Couldn't you see what you were doing to me? I couldn't speak, I couldn't breathe."

And how had he felt? "Stunned" didn't even begin to cover it. He could never have been prepared for seeing Beth again, he realised now. "You made a great presentation."

She ignored his attempt to return to safer ground. "I couldn't think straight…not with you staring at me."

"I was listening to you." He was trying to stay calm, but for the first time in his life something inside him snapped. "Do you think I want to look at you? Do you think I want my mind full of you when I should be thinking about my country? Do you think I should be here, while my people wait for me in Q'Adar?"

"So why *are* you here, Khal?"

"I think you know."

Pressing her lips together as if she didn't trust herself to speak, she shook her head.

"I'm here for you," he told her bluntly, tiring of the act.

"What? You're here for me? Oh, Khal, please!"

She gave a short, angry laugh that spoke of all the hurt inside her. "What happened to all those other women?"

"Other women?"

"Here, look at them." From under the pile of documents, she took a magazine and thrust it at him. "Take a look at that and then tell me again why you're here."

He only had to look at the first one. "When tensions began to heighten in Q'Adar, my first thought was to divert attention from you. Clumsily, now, it seems."

"Yes," she said, sounding bitterly hurt. She glanced at the headline on the cover and read it out loud to him. "'Princess Layla comforts the ruler of Q'Adar on one of his rare breaks from leading his army against the insurgents'... Or what about this one? 'The Sultana Lydia enters negotiations for an arms deal with the warrior sheikh'... A clever play on words, don't you think, Khal?" Snatching the magazine from him, she flung it on the floor at his feet.

"What better way is there to get a message across than through the media?" he said grimly. "I was trying to protect you, and I could hardly make an announcement on the news. Those women were nothing more than props."

"Props?" Beth's mouth worked. "And what am I, Khal?"

"You're the woman I want."

"Just like that—you decide? After all these weeks, *you* decide?"

"You…" He searched for words that properly expressed his feelings. "Preoccupied my mind."

"You mean you want sex?"

"No!" The word exploded from him. "Don't demean yourself. I left a country enduring the birth pangs to come here for you. And I came the first moment I could get away."

"So now you want me—as what?" she said in a small voice. "As your mistress?"

He stared at her intently. "And you don't want that?"

She flinched. "No, I don't want that."

"But I want you. Only you…"

It was as his mother had told her, Beth thought helplessly; she could be as strong as she liked, but the invisible bond between the ruler of Q'Adar and the Liverpool shop girl would never break. Closing her eyes, she inhaled sharply, and when

Khal reached for her and slowly pulled her towards him she didn't resist. She was strong enough for most things, but not for this. As heat rose up inside her he backed her oh, so slowly towards the door. She was sure her legs would crumple beneath her before they reached it, and when they did she gasped with relief, hearing Khal slip the lock. He started kissing her, gently, tenderly, on the brow and on the eyes, and on the lips and on her neck, keeping her moving all the time, backing her towards the desk until she felt the smooth wood pressing against the top of her legs.

The desktop was at the perfect height. Grasping the lapels of his jacket, she pushed it from his shoulders. As it fell to the floor she reached for the buckle on his belt, and unfastened it. Loosening his tie, she freed the buttons at the neck of his shirt, excited even more by the sight of the familiar smooth, bronze skin with its shading of dark hair. Moving on, she released the catch on his pants and undid the zip. That was the signal for Khal to drag her to him and kiss her with a savage intensity that matched her own. When he released her she tugged his trousers down and wriggled free of her briefs. He nudged his way between her thighs before they even hit the floor. She felt him grow bigger, harder, in her hands.

"How much of me do you want?"

"All of you," she commanded hoarsely, throwing back her head. "I want all of you," she gasped as Khal plunged deep.

It was so much more pleasure than she remembered. It was amazing. She screamed out, not caring who might hear her. And once wasn't enough. Once wasn't nearly enough. She moved fiercely while Khal worked his hips, just as she wanted him to, until finally she slumped exhausted in his arms. "You don't need me?" he said.

She didn't answer.

They took a long, warm shower in the small private bathroom, but even there they couldn't keep away from each other. She was frantic for him, like a man without water in the desert who had found a well. With Khal's arms braced against the tiled walls, and her legs locked around his waist, their shower had turned cold without them realising it, and she was trembling with exhaustion again by the time Khal lowered her to the ground.

"Finished?" he teased against her lips.

"It has to be enough, I've got work to do."

"Work?" His voice changed. He pulled away. "Work will have to wait."

"It can't wait."

"I haven't come all this way to stand in line. You've got the rest of the day off."

It was a stark reminder of who he was, but she wasn't up for being steamrollered. "I can't. I've got a duty."

"To me," Khal cut across her flatly.

"No." Beth shook her head as she stepped out of the shower and took the towel he handed her. "I won't just disappear, Khal, and let people down. I'm expected."

"Don't worry about it. Everyone knows you won't be available for the rest of the day."

"You told them that?" Beth pressed her lips together angrily. "I can't believe you just arrived and took over my life."

Rather than rise to her anger, Khal's lips tugged wryly. "I know no other way. You'll have to teach me…"

She was stopped in her tracks. Khal had taken the wind right out of her sails. But was he serious? And then his hard face softened even more. "Won't you show me round your city, Beth?"

He never got the chance to do anything ordinary, she realised. "Really?" she said, still suspicious of his motives. "The guided tour?"

"If you'll take me."

As he smiled, she softened. "Just you and me?"

"Absolutely."

"No outriders?"

"No limousine, no outriders, no Sheikh. Just Beth Tracey Torrance and Khal from Q'Adar."

"Like normal people?" Beth made a small huff of disbelief.

"It's not impossible, is it?"

Impossible? No. It was sad, Beth realised. She showed nothing on her face, but she was thinking—one of the most powerful men in the world was asking her to show him what "normal" was, and what ordinary people did on an ordinary day out. There would be no yachts or helicopters, and no armed guards, just an open-top bus and the two of them. She could fight Khal all she liked, but the idea he'd put forward was irresistible to someone who cared about him as much as she did. "If you're sure you really want to…"

"I really do," he said, and the look he gave her made her heart melt. Having made her decision, she tipped her chin and looked him over. "In that case, I'd better find you something comfortable to wear..."

"So what does his Majesty think of the open-top bus ride?"

"Khal."

As he prompted her, Beth tried to ignore the feelings in her heart. This was going nowhere—except to the bus terminal—and it was time she faced up to that fact. But finding a way to stop her heart hammering with love for him was another thing.

She was so lovely it almost blinded him to look at her. He had wanted this time alone with her. He counted it as precious, private time away from other people, and valued it more than Beth would ever know. However hard he'd tried, he couldn't let her go. He *wouldn't* let her go. She wasn't interested in his wealth or his position, or even the fact that he was one of the most powerful men in the Arab world and beyond. She was tender and true, and quirky. She was also the hottest thing on two spectacular legs. Bottom line—if he wanted Beth Tracey Torrance, he had to play at least part of the game by her rules.

She grinned at him, and then the rain hit them both in the face.

"Okay, so maybe we'll get off here," he said, tugging off the jacket she'd found for him in the store to drape it round her shoulders. The jeans and shirt she'd picked out for him wouldn't come to harm, but he didn't want Beth getting wet.

He ushered her off the bus when it reached Albert Dock. He knew she wanted to look round the Tate. She stood entranced in the gallery in front of some stunning, contemporary Chinese art. The trip was a great success, and she was relaxed by the time he took her for lunch in the café. She had a hearty appetite in all departments, but it was her enthusiasm for life that attracted him the most. As she dabbed her lips with the napkin, she drew his attention to how deliciously full they were, and how much he wanted to kiss her again.

"That was delicious, and I'm stuffed," she claimed happily, without a care in the world.

"Wonderful," he said. "I only want to see you happy."

Before he had chance to say any more, she interrupted him. "I can't believe I managed three courses. I never do that. But deep-fried potatoes with chilli sauce are my absolute favourites."

"Along with tuna Niçoise, and chocolate pudding with chocolate sauce, I assume?"

"Absolutely," she agreed. "Sorry, I interrupted you. What were you about to say?" She gazed at him intently.

"I've got something to show you," he said. "Not that," he murmured when she gave him a look full of mischief.

"What is it? Will I like it?"

"You'll just have to come with me, if you want to find out…" And this time when he held out his hand to her she took hold of it trustingly.

CHAPTER EIGHT

"WHAT are you doing?" Beth said when Khal flipped out his mobile and started punching in numbers. They had stopped outside the entrance to the Tate.

"Calling the cavalry..."

"You promised me no outriders." She felt her stomach sink. "I thought this was going to be a normal day?"

"And so it is," he assured her.

"For you or for me?"

"Don't get mad, or you won't get your surprise."

"Okay." Beth bit back on her disappointment. "I'll give you a chance, but only one, mind."

With a grin that made her stomach lurch, Khal silenced her before speaking in Arabic to his driver.

"So, where are we going?" she asked him as the limousine pulled up at the kerb.

"To my penthouse in the city."

"You are full of surprises."

"You don't have to come with me," he said, reaching for the door handle.

"But you're sure I will," she commented dryly as Khal waved his chauffeur aside and helped her into the car. "I suppose it won't hurt me to see where you hang out."

"And maybe linger a while?" he suggested, climbing in beside her.

"You always have the best ideas," Beth agreed, wondering if it would always be like this between them, the sexual tension reaching danger-levels constantly—but with a man driving them that wasn't good. She noticed both she and Khal were making sure they kept a good space between them on the spacious back seat.

Khal's penthouse was fabulous. A massive, high-ceilinged, oak-floored entrance hall complete with life-sized sculptures led through to a modern and sophisticated open-plan living area. There were panoramic views across the city and the estuary to the Welsh hills beyond, through the floor-to-ceiling window. As far as Beth was concerned every superlative she had in her head was totally inadequate to describe it, and so she settled for, "Wow!"

"So you like it?"

"And I thought I'd seen everything in Q'Adar!" she exclaimed, turning full-circle. "What's not to like? How big is this place?"

"Around five thousand."

"Square feet?" Beth demanded in astonishment. "And you keep this just for when you visit Liverpool?" When Khal didn't answer her right away, alarms bells started ringing in her head. She noticed now that there was none of the usual personal stuff around. She decided to probe a little. "I love it, but it's not exactly what I'd call a home," she said innocently.

"Not yet," Khal agreed, "But you could soon change that."

"I could change it? Go on!" Beth gave a short laugh. "You're kidding me." The idea of her putting her stamp on a place like this was beyond even her wildest flights of imagination.

"No. I'm absolutely serious," Khal assured her. "Would you care to tour the master suite?"

Her body was still throbbing from his lovemaking, and it didn't take much to turn her thoughts in the direction of the master suite. Time to put her suspicions to one side. The time they'd spent apart had made her greedy for Khal. As if sensing this, he touched her, running the knuckles of one hand lightly down her arm, and then he reached for her so that now she was operating on a purely sensual plane with no thought of where this was leading. Burrowing her face in his strong, warm neck felt so good and so right, and the next thing she knew Khal had swung her into his arms. Shouldering his way through one of the doors, he took her into the most amazing bedroom—though she hardly had time to notice all the blonde wood, glass and mirrors before he laid her gently on the bed and stripped off her clothes. Joining her without a suggestion of embarrassment, he stretched out next to her. "You have an incredible body," she said, running her fingertips over his smooth, bronze skin.

His face softened as he looked at her. "And you're beautiful," he said, kissing, stroking, and reassuring her.

He wanted Beth to feel like the most cherished woman on the face of the earth, which was how he felt about her. Yes, he wanted her, but each time he brought her into his arms it was as if his world exploded with possibilities. Kissing her tenderly, he cupped her face and stared into her eyes, and what he saw there told him she felt the same.

They made love until the setting sun had thrown its last dart into the estuary, and reflection off the glass had bathed the room in crimson light. They slept a little, and when Beth finally woke it was to find Khal staring down at her. "What?" she murmured, groggily, reaching up to touch his face.

"I was just thinking," he said softly, "that I can't wait for you to take a proper look around the apartment, and see if you could be happy here..."

Frowning as she tried to compute Khal's words, Beth tried to stop him getting out of bed. "Do we have to do that now?"

"I'm impatient," he said. "I just want to be sure you like it before I sign it over to you."

"Before you *what*?" She was fully awake now.

Khal looked at her. "Why are you so surprised?"

"I would have thought that was obvious," she said. "I don't want a penthouse. I don't want anything from you." She could tell from the expression on Khal's face that she might have been talking gibberish, but then he never had seen the gulf between them. Slipping out of bed, she grabbed a robe. "You can't hand over a property to me as if it's a sweater you're tired of!"

"I'm not tired of it, I bought it for you."

"You bought it for *me*?" Beth clutched the top of her head as if she had to contain all the confused thoughts jostling inside there. "Are you mad?"

Khal ignored this. "It's a good investment," he said, swinging out of bed. "But, if you don't like it, we'll look for something else."

"I don't want anything else—I don't want this—"

"You must have somewhere suitable to live."

"Why must I?" Beth's hackles rose as the penny dropped. "What do you mean 'somewhere suitable', Khal?" she said tightly. "I already have a house."

"And where is it?"

As Khal's drew himself up, she felt like stamping on his toes to bring him down to earth. Okay, her small modern townhouse wasn't a palace or a penthouse like this, but it was her home. And there were special reasons why it meant so much to her. She had received a surprise legacy on her twenty-first birthday from the father she'd never known. She had stared at the cheque when it had arrived from the solicitors for a long time, knowing she would have given it back in a second to know her father, and that it was too late. She wasn't about to throw that away as if it meant nothing. "My home might not be what you're used to," she told Khal. "But it's all mine. Well, mine and the mortgage company's."

"And this penthouse could be yours without a mortgage."

"If I agree to what?"

She stood there with a look of anger and disappointment on her face. "For goodness" sake, Beth! I'm giving you a penthouse. How much more can you ask of me?"

And there was the rub, Beth thought sadly. Khal wanted to give her so much in the monetary sense, but in her eyes his gift was valueless.

"If you want something bigger—something with a proper garden—"

"Khal, stop this! I don't need expensive gifts

from you. That's not what I want—" Beth stopped in case her feelings for him poured out.

"Then what do you want?" he demanded with exasperation.

They were so far apart in outlook, in everything that really mattered, he would never understand. She settled for, "My house suits me fine, and I don't need anywhere else to live."

"We'll discuss this when you've calmed down."

"No, we won't," Beth said firmly. "Where I live isn't up for negotiation."

"But things have changed now."

"What's changed? What do you mean, things have changed *now*? Oh, I see," Beth said as the penny dropped. "You're assuming that wherever I live can't possibly be upmarket enough for the ruler of Q'Adar to visit when he's in town..."

"That's not what I said."

"It's what you meant, though." Firming her lips, Beth turned away. She didn't know when she had felt so hurt. "If you think I'm going to become your mistress—"

"Think again?"

Khal's face had turned colder than Beth had ever seen it, and though she could never agree to this it was a stark reminder that people devoted their lives to the ruler of Q'Adar, and considered themselves fortunate to be able to do so.

She only had herself to blame for falling in love with him, Beth thought, hugging herself unhappily as she turned away. And she was twice the fool for imagining Khal might love her. "I can't do this, Khal." She could never agree to become just another one of his possessions. "I can never be the woman you want me to be."

Beth wondered why it was so quiet, and why Khal hadn't answered her. When she turned, she saw he was on his way to take a shower. She felt a chill pass over her as he paused and turned to face her at the door. "There's another bathroom over there," he said, pointing across the room. "Use it and then let yourself out."

Her jaw dropped. For once she was lost for words. She was stunned, angry, hurt, bewildered…and, most of all, full of grief and loss. How could a life that had felt so full only moments before feel so empty now? How had this happened? How had she allowed this to happen? How in her wildest dreams had she imagined the ruler of Q'Adar could ever love her as she loved him? Burying her head in her hands, Beth realised that her overriding feeling was shame. Everything in Khal's life came easily to him, and she had made herself available like all the rest. So much for all those brave thoughts at the ball—she had fallen into bed with him as eagerly as any of the other women there might have done. And now...? It had taken a single act of defiance on her part for Khal to discard her like a pair of ill-fitting shoes.

His timing was out. Everything was out. His world was off-kilter. How else could he explain exiting his bathroom at the same time as Beth? He was still battling his internal demons, wondering where he'd gone wrong. He'd bought her the best property in the whole of Liverpool and she'd rejected him. *She* had rejected *him*. "My apologies," he heard himself say stiffly. "I thought you would have gone home by now."

"It's usual in Liverpool for a host to make sure their guest gets home safely," she told him tightly, with not one iota of her courage stripped away. "Can you call a taxi, or shall I?"

Her steady gaze shamed him. He was so accustomed to having a car at the kerb everywhere he went, it hadn't occurred to him to call a taxi for Beth. And it was dark outside now. What had he been thinking? "Of course I'll call a taxi for you." His voice reflected anger with himself, but she wasn't to know that. "Or you could use my car."

One taupe brow rose. "A taxi will be fine for me, thank you." Her lips pressed together as she held his gaze.

For once he didn't know what to say and just made the call. He had been confident of her enthusiasm for his scheme. He had believed this to be the perfect solution. "What's wrong with you, Beth?" he said as soon as he finished the call.

"What's wrong with me? No, don't answer that," she told him. "I know what's wrong with me. I'm naïve—and that's just for starters."

"You must have known—"

"Why you brought me here? You're right, I should have known. I should have expected it, because that's all I am to you."

"Beth," he warned.

"Don't 'Beth' me!"

"Look what I'm offering you…"

"You're offering me nothing," she said angrily.

"And the saddest thing of all is you can't see it. You've killed off any hope of a future we ever had today. You've suffocated my love for you beneath your gross gift of a fabulously expensive penthouse, when an ice cream would have made me happy."

"Don't be so ridiculous! I'll buy you anything you want."

"But not this!" She gestured wildly, crying now. "You're trying to buy me, Khal, and I can't be bought. You think you're offering me a million-pound home, while I think you're trying to turn my life into a theme park for you to dip into whenever you feel like playing at being an ordinary person. But when you tire of that, Khal, when you don your crown and forget about me, what am I supposed to do then?"

"I'll never forget you. And your life won't change."

"My life won't change?" She spoke slowly and deliberately, annunciating each word as if she had to be sure of his meaning. "You're even more cut off from reality than I thought."

"And you're overreacting," he said impatiently, turning away. He had never felt like this, his insides churning. He had never felt so unsettled and dissatisfied before. They waited out a tense silence until the bell sounded on the intercom. "That will be your taxi," he said unnecessarily, walking her to the door.

"Don't bother coming down with me," she said in a clipped voice. "I'll be just fine."

He didn't doubt it, but would he?

If she had slept for even a second she might have thought twice before lifting the phone when it started ringing.

"Beth?" The voice was expressionless, but unmistakeable.

"Yes, it's me…" She held her breath and then said what had to be said. "I haven't changed my mind, Khal, and I think it's better if we don't see each other again."

"You took the words right out of my mouth."

"Oh…" Somehow she wasn't prepared for that. Biting her lip, Beth squeezed the phone until she had proper control of herself. "Why are you calling, then?"

"I just wanted to set your mind at ease before I leave the country, and tell you that whatever happened between us will not impact on your future with Khalifa."

She remained silent. If he'd expected enthusiasm, he was out of luck.

"Yes, in fact I have recommended you for promotion."

"I wish you hadn't."

"This has nothing to do with us. You're the best person for the job, and that's all there is to it."

"Thank you." She felt numb.

"Well, that's it… Maybe I'll see you next time?"

"Maybe…"

There was just the suggestion of a pause, and then the line went dead.

CHAPTER NINE

GRIPPING on to the cold white porcelain in her small *en suite,* Beth wondered if she was going to be sick again. As the moment passed, and she was capable of doing things again without worrying she was going to faint, she ran a basin full of cold water and dunked her face in it. Emerging spluttering, she felt clean, fresher, and more determined than ever. She knew what she had to do; she wasn't the type to let things hang.

She called into the chemist on her way to work, and then took refuge in the staff bathroom to carry out the simple test and wait for the result. She emerged from the bathroom a different person from the woman who had gone in; something deep inside her had just adjusted to a new orbit.

She was excited and scared and overwhelmed by the complications and consequences of carrying Khal's baby. But more than anything love was everywhere, bursting out of her, exploding in a cascade of shimmering light. If only she'd had someone to share it with. The love she felt for the baby they'd made was overwhelming, and her love for Khal was constant. Fate had played a cunning hand. Khal could never legitimise their relationship, but they were tied together now for the rest of their lives. She must do the right thing and let him know.

She tried first to contact him through the embassy, but no one would release his private telephone number, even when Beth explained in a small white lie that she was a member of his staff.

It was too late now to wonder why she hadn't asked for his number before, Beth reflected as she replaced the telephone receiver in its nest. And far too late for shame at the thought that if she had asked Khal for his number he probably wouldn't have given it to her, even though in every other way they'd been intimate. Even so, it was a miracle she had become pregnant. She wasn't on the Pill, but Khal had always been careful to use contraception.

It was no use looking back, Beth told herself firmly, and about as much use blaming the manufacturers of contraceptives as it was panicking

about the future. This was her baby and her responsibility, and she would cope as she always
had. She adored her baby already, and felt fiercely
protective of it; she would guard it with her life.

Full of resolve she rang the embassy again, and
this time left a message for His Majesty to call
her back. It drew a sharp intake of breath from
the person on the other end of the line, and wasn't
really satisfactory for Beth—but she could hardly
blurt out the fact that she was pregnant by the
ruler of Q'Adar to a stranger. The only person
she would give that news to was Khal. And she'd
have to do that discreetly. She had seen enough in
the gossip magazines to know how young women
were derided for pointing the finger at wealthy
men. And Khal was more than wealthy. She had
nothing to lose, but what about her baby? No
child of hers was going to be exposed to ridicule.

For now she would go back to work, Beth decided. It was crucial she brought in an income.
There was the future to think about, a future in
which her child might not grow up to know the
trappings of great wealth, but they would know
love. It would be safer for them to live quietly
and anonymously, so that was what she would do.

Beth did everything required of her that day at work and more. If what Khal said was true and she was in line for a promotion, then she was determined to prove herself worthy of that promotion ten times over. She was dead on her feet by the time a phone call came through for her. She took it by the till in the store, expecting it to be one of her loyal customers wanting her to put something aside for them.

"Ms Torrance?"

Beth's heart stopped. The accent if not the voice was unmistakeable. "Yes...?"

"I am calling from the Q'Adaran embassy, Ms Torrance."

If she could have fast-forwarded the conversation she would have done—right up to the part where the man said, "His Majesty regrets..."

He regretted? Regretted what? Beth shrank inside. What now? She had to make herself concentrate on what the man was saying to her. "Keys?" she said in confusion. "I don't know about any keys."

"To the penthouse, Ms Torrance."

"I'm sorry?"

"His Majesty has signed over the deeds of a

property, which I believe you have viewed? I'm arranging to have the keys couriered to your home address."

Beth recoiled. "I don't want it."

"I'm sorry, Ms Torrance, but that's something your lawyer will have to take up with our legal department."

"I need to speak to him—to Khal—to His Majesty, I mean. It's really important." Beth hardly knew that she was nursing her still-flat stomach in a protective way as she spoke. "Can you give me a number where I can reach him?"

"I'm sorry, Ms Torrance, I'm not at liberty to release that information."

"Then can you put me through to someone who can get a message through?"

"I'm sorry, Ms Torrance," the caller repeated patiently. "That won't be possible."

"If someone could just tell him that I called…"

"In the event that you called, His Majesty has already left instructions that no thanks are necessary."

Beth had to silence the hysterical laughter bubbling up inside her. And now it was too late, because the line had cut. Khal couldn't have made it any clearer that he didn't want to talk to her, and, whether she wanted it or not, he had given her the penthouse as a pay-off. And also as a reminder, just in case she had forgotten, that the ruler of Q'Adar pulled everyone's strings.

There was nothing she could do about it, Beth realised, firming her lips. She felt angrily defensive on behalf of her baby. Khal wasn't going to pull their strings. She would bring up their child without his help, and in her own home, and not one of his choosing. She would call a lawyer now, because she needed someone to advise her on the best way to rent out the penthouse and invest the money for her child. She wouldn't touch a penny of the money it brought in, but it would provide security for her baby in the future.

"It's about time you went home, isn't it?" the elderly doorman joked as Beth smiled goodbye to him. "You look terrible."

"Thank you," Beth replied wryly. Wasn't that what she needed to hear after the day she'd had? But, not being the type to cower in a corner, she came straight out with it. "I probably look pale because I'm pregnant."

To his credit her old friend barely missed a beat. "It can hit some women like that in the first few months. If you need any advice, I'll put you in touch with my wife—she's had seven."

"That's really kind of you, but my mother—" Beth swallowed hard and carried on with the deception "—can't wait to share her experiences with me."

"There's nothing like having your family behind you."

"No, there isn't, is there?" Beth smiled brightly, knowing it was better for the sake of discretion if everyone thought she had everything firmly under control.

Hana Katie Torrance was born smiling after a relatively easy birth, and went on to become the first baby to enter the new crèche at the luxurious Khalifa store in Liverpool. Hana meant "happiness" in Arabic, which was how Beth had felt about her baby from the first moment she had discovered she was pregnant. And that feeling had developed wings since the day she'd felt her baby stir inside her. Hana's birth had been the brightest day of her life. And life was good for

Beth's small family in her cosy, loving home, a family that now included Faith, a friend from school, who had come to Khalifa in hope of a position as a nursery nurse at the new crèche. It had made sense to both girls for Faith to move in with Beth and Hana and work part-time at the store.

Yes, life was good, Beth reflected with a sigh, as she prepared for work that morning. And she couldn't think of one way to improve it, other than to rid herself of the longing in her heart, the longing that had never lessened, even though it had been over a year since she'd last seen Khal.

Longing for things she couldn't have was a bad habit she'd have to lose, Beth told herself firmly as she packed Hana's bag for the day. "Baby wipes, nappies, food and toys—all present and correct," she told Faith, glancing distractedly at the television news. There had been more troubles in Q'Adar, where the corrupt old sheikhs were unwilling to let go of their power. The news reporter said everything was quiet now, and that the ruling sheikh was firmly back in control. Beth bit her lip as she worried about Khal. She would always worry about him, even though she hadn't heard from him in all this time. Did he know he had a baby daughter? And, if he did, would he care? Surely someone must have told him? Glancing at the clock, Beth realised it was time to leave.

There were no happy endings outside of fairy tales, Beth reminded herself on the way to the store. The ruler of Q'Adar would hardly be interested in a Liverpool shop-girl when he had the ruling of a turbulent country on his mind.

"Shall I take our little princess?" Faith asked, jolting Beth back into the real world, their world, as they walked along the road. She hadn't told Faith the whole story, and thankfully Faith had never pushed for information, sensing something of Beth's inner grief.

"Hana *is* our princess, isn't she?" Beth said, smiling. She thought back to the hours immediately after childbirth when she'd been alone. She'd picked up a hand mirror and seen this fat, frumpy, plain woman, and had thought to herself that Khal had had a narrow escape. But plain or not she was going to throw everything she had into making Hana happy. And look what he was missing, Beth thought as she stopped to tenderly transfer Hana into Faith's arms at the door of the store. All the money and power in the world couldn't compare to this precious gift.

Beth thought a lot about Khal that day, and the dangers he was facing. She knew he would quell them, because she knew Khal. She knew he would never give up or back down, and that the wellbeing of his people meant everything to him. But when everything was back to normal in Q'Adar she wouldn't want to be part of that glittering, empty world, and it wasn't what she wanted for Hana either. And then a thought struck Beth that chilled her to the bone. What if, when the country was settled, Khal decided he wanted Hana in Q'Adar? What if he married one of those haughty princesses and then wanted Hana with them? His glamorous new wife was bound to look down on the daughter of a shop girl...

Beth couldn't bear to think about it. She couldn't bear to think of Hana being treated like a second-class citizen, or joining a family where she wasn't wanted. It must never come to that, she determined, and while she had breath in her body it never would.

* * *

He couldn't pretend he was back in Liverpool more than a year down the road just to tour the store. He didn't give a reason. He didn't need to. This was more than a business visit, it was an imperative. When he'd taken over in Q'Adar he'd had no idea how far the bribery and corruption had spread. In the absence of a strong leader, intrigue had spread like a malignant disease. No one had expected him to stamp down on it so fast when he came to power. The corrupt sheikhs had underestimated him, and they had underestimated his response. He had a kingdom and a people to defend, and he would do that in spite of threats against him and his family. He refused to be intimidated, but this was the first chance he'd had to get away and bring the rest of his family under his protection. Beth was part of his family now, whether she chose to be or not.

He left the limousine a few blocks away from his destination, telling his bodyguards to keep their distance. He needed space and time to think, luxuries usually denied him. He knew everything there was to know about Beth Tracey Torrance and their baby daughter, Hana. He'd had daily reports delivered to him whenever he'd been in Q'Adar. He'd known almost to the hour when Beth had discovered she was pregnant, and had set up a protection squad to keep her safe. The enormity of his responsibilities in Q'Adar had kept him there, but he had followed his baby daughter's progress with the keenest interest. He was pleased that Beth had called their daughter Hana. Even a little thing like a name would make his daughter's transition into her life as an Arabian princess that much easier.

Noting the undercover agents as he walked past them, he quickened his step. He was eager to see his child...eager to see Beth. And more than anything he was eager to get them both back to Q'Adar where he could ensure their safety. The uprising was over, but he couldn't protect them from renegades who might seek them out in England. And there was another reason. His people had placed their trust in him, and he wanted to repay that trust by marrying a suitable woman and providing his people with continuity—which meant providing them with an heir. It was essential that Hana was settled in Q'Adar before he married. Her presence in the palace would establish her as a member of the royal family, making her position in his affections clear before his new bride came to live there.

A year was a long time. He felt a rush of excitement as he entered the store. Surveillance photographs had told him something about Beth, and he was sure her resilience and humour were still in place—but what changes in her would he find, if any?

For instance, would motherhood soften her attitude towards becoming his mistress now that concern for baby Hana must override her pride?

He had dreamed of this moment for months, Khal realised, choosing to run up the escalator rather than wait for the lift. But would his feisty little Beth take to life in Q'Adar, even once he was married? He knew the answer to that before he even asked her the question.

He winced as he caught sight of his reflection in a mirror as he strode through her department, longing for a glimpse of her. How would she feel about seeing him battled-scarred and hardened? How would Beth feel about him?

Settling Hana in her cot at the crèche, Beth felt the change in the air before she saw anything, and the shiver down her back confirmed she was right to be frightened. Her first instinct was to reach for Hana, pick her up, and hold her tight.

"Beth…"

As she froze he thought the image of Beth holding their baby would never leave him, and he felt a great swell of emotion seeing them together for the first time. Her instinct was to shield her baby, and as she turned he saw the fear in her eyes. But, even so, she surprised him with her quick thinking and composure.

"Ring me if you need me," she said calmly to a girl in nurse's uniform who was obviously on duty that morning in the babies" darkened sleep-room.

"Don't worry, I will," the girl said, looking curiously at him.

Beth braced herself and turned around. "Hello, Khal…" Nothing could have prepared her for seeing him again. All the warnings in the world wouldn't have been enough. In essence he was the same, but there were lines of strain around his eyes and his mouth, and recent scars on his face. Had it only been just over a year? A year in which her world had been turned upside down—but then so had Khal's, and in a different, ugly way.

"May I?" he said.

She recognised that tone in his voice. It echoed her own sense of wonder whenever Hana was in view. "Of course," she said. She would never stop him seeing his daughter, but she had feared this moment most of all. "So, you knew…"

"Of course I knew," Khal murmured, nursing his daughter.

Of course he knew. That was the power he wielded. And as Khal stared into Hana's face Beth feared that this was not the tender lover she'd known who had returned on a visit—but a warrior fresh from a war, a man who had come to claim his child.

CHAPTER TEN

THERE were so many unanswered questions, but all Beth was aware of was a creeping sense of dread. There was such intensity in Khal's gaze as he stared down at their baby daughter. She understood it, but it frightened her. There was a sense of loss too, lodged in the pit of her stomach like a heavy weight. Her feelings for Khal were unchanged, but that sense of loss was for something that had never been hers.

Oblivious to these undercurrents between her parents, Hana woke. The bond between father and daughter was instantaneous. Stretching out her tiny hand, Hana claimed Khal, curling her palm around his index finger. The look on his face transformed him, and when he smiled back at Hana Beth knew for certain that all their lives must change for good now. Instinct drove her to take up position on the opposite side of the cot to Khal, where she remained like a lioness in defence of its cub. Since Khal's shock appearance she hadn't been thinking straight, but she was acutely alert now. She had to keep her wits about her. Khal was supremely powerful, and used to wielding that power. If he decided to walk out with Hana, what could she do? And if he took their baby to Q'Adar would she ever see Hana again? The only thing left to her was to open a line of communication between them. "Say hello to your daddy, Hana," Beth said, hoping this might touch Khal's icy heart.

"Hana's a baby," he said impatiently, "and she can't speak yet." Lifting his head, he gave Beth an admonishing stare. "And when you address a royal child you should remember that baby-talk is inappropriate."

Beth recoiled inwardly. Was this something he'd learned in the royal nursery at Q'Adar? She couldn't imagine it had come from his mother: from a nurse, perhaps. But didn't a baby love the tone of its parent's voice, and couldn't it hear the affection and love? Was that wrong now? As Khal turned his back on her Beth felt like she had been slapped in the face. She didn't have a model for parenting, and had done her best using instinct. That instinct was telling her now that Khal had just reinforced their respective positions in life, and that he was going to take Hana to the opposite side of the great divide. She spared a reassuring glance for Faith, who was doing her best to seem invisible, and then moved deeper into the shadows where she and Khal could talk discreetly. She beckoned him over. His dark eyes queried her impertinence at ordering him, but she stood her ground until he joined her. She told him straight. "Please don't inflict your cold, unfeeling ways on Hana."

Khal's eyes were like black diamonds, hard and unmoving. "You'll do as *I* say where our daughter is concerned."

"*Our* daughter," Beth whispered, trying to remind him that she had a say. But she also had to remember that this was a man who had lived his entire life without emotion, a man whose world was not a cosy home but a palace, a man who had come here fresh from subduing his opponents. She had to find a way to make him see that this was a very different situation, and to do that she had to swallow a bucketful of pride. "Khal, I'm begging you..."

"Not here." He glanced at Faith. "In my office; five minutes."

Inwardly Beth was furious, but she would show none of that in front of Hana. She might be a mouse confronting the hawk of the desert, but when it came to their child Khal must learn that she would fight. "I'm going to settle Hana back in her cot first," she said, reaching for her, "and then I'll come to your office."

"Can't the nurse do that?"

Beth didn't answer. She remained where she was with her arms outstretched, waiting for her child; she wasn't going anywhere until Khal passed Hana over.

"There can be no agreement between us while you make these insane demands," Beth argued. She was standing rigid with disbelief in the office Khal had taken over for his visit. He had insisted she must return immediately with him to Q'Adar and forget her life in England. "I can't just throw everything up. I have a job here, responsibilities—"

"Yes," he cut across her. "Responsibilities, to me and to your daughter."

She knew she didn't count, but the expression on Khal's face cut Beth out of the picture completely. He wanted his daughter, and if he couldn't part Beth from Hana then she must come too; that was what it amounted to. Her heart ached for the closeness they'd known, and for Khal too, but this was not the time for her to soften. It was crucial to meet Khal's steel with steel, or she'd go down. No chance *that* was going to happen with Hana to protect. Khal might be a slave to duty and cut off from emotion, but she was a mother devoted to her child. "You can't uproot Hana on a whim. She has a routine."

"Which can be reinstated in Q'Adar—and this is not a whim. I'm here because the safety of our daughter is at stake."

"Hana's safety?" Beth felt sick. The world as she knew it was disintegrating, and taking its place was something frightening and unknown. The rights and wrongs of going with Khal were irrelevant. Her whole concentration was focused on keeping Hana safe. "What do you mean?" she whispered.

"I intended to explain that to you on our flight back to Q'Adar."

"You thought I would come with you meekly and without question?"

"I thought you would trust me."

Beth's gaze flickered. "It's not enough, Khal. I must know what you mean before I make a decision like this for Hana."

"The situation in Q'Adar is turbulent and unpredictable."

"All the more reason for staying here."

"No," he said firmly. "I cannot guarantee Hana's safety when she's so far away from me. The troubles in Q'Adar are like the random thrashings of a mad dog in the final throes of its agony. We are close to stamping it out, but there are those who bear grudges and would try to slip away to try and distract me from my purpose. They would stab me in my heart," he said bitterly.

"Your heart?" The look in Khal's eyes stopped Beth making any more remarks along those lines. Hana had released something inside him he had been frightened of admitting, even to himself— that not only did Khal have a heart, but he was capable of love so instant, so deep and lasting, it had taken even him by surprise.

"There can be no delay. I have made my decision."

"*You* have made a decision?" Beth said, refocusing. "Hana has two parents."

"What are you doing?" he said, snatching a phone out of her hand.

"Calling my lawyer." Thank goodness she had appointed one, along with all the other precautions she had taken, like obtaining a passport for Hana so they would never be trapped anywhere by anyone.

"And alert my enemies? There isn't time for you to call a lawyer and book an appointment for some time next week. This is an urgent matter."

"For you, but I must consider all Hana's options. I need time to think."

"There is no time to think. We don't have that luxury. I can assure you I wouldn't have come unless there was real and pressing danger. I came to you the instant the situation in Q'Adar was under control, but when you're here I can't protect you both properly."

"If you'd told me, if you'd explained, if you'd even given me some warning…"

He made a dismissive gesture. "I don't expect

you to understand. You're still living in your small, safe world—or at least that's what you think. That world can change horribly and in an instant, Beth. Do you want to be alone when it does?"

For the first time Beth wasn't sure what to say.

"You must accept that our daughter inhabits the same world stage as her father."

"From which I am excluded?"

"You don't face the same risks," Khal said flatly.

And would she put Hana at risk? Her options had dwindled to nothing, Beth realised. Hana's safety was paramount. Did she have any alternative but to go with Khal? "If you can keep Hana safe," she murmured tensely, speaking her thoughts out loud.

"I can," Khal told her. "If she returns with me now to Q'Adar. But I cannot secure the rest of the world for you, Beth. You must come back with me."

Closing her eyes for a moment, Beth begged for guidance. "Then I will," she agreed on a shuddering breath. She could only pray she'd done the right thing.

* * *

And do what when she arrived in Q'Adar? Beth wondered as she packed their day bag hurriedly and explained as best she could to Faith. Would she live out her life in Q'Adar as a second-class citizen, the ruling sheikh's embarrassing little secret? How would that affect Hana's future? Would Hana grow up estranged from her in a different part of the palace? Would she be forced to endure taunts and insults in later life because her mother was deemed unworthy? Beth bit her lip at the thought of Hana suffering in any way. "There's no other alternative to this, is there?" Beth confirmed with Khal as they left the building. "You couldn't leave more guards here to keep Hana safe?" She hesitated outside the limousine with Hana in her arms.

"You think you live in a warm, safe nest," Khal told her. "But what you forget is that violence can follow you everywhere. It can seep through the cracks of your happy life and steal everything you care about away."

"Is that meant to frighten me into coming with you?"

"Beth…" Khal's jaw worked as he fought back his feelings, and for just a second Beth thought she saw his eyes change too; they seemed to soften with understanding. "I wish that was all it was with all my heart."

Gazing at Hana, Beth knew she couldn't remain stubbornly obstinate; she had to do what was right for her baby.

Trouble started on the journey to the airport when questions bombarded Beth's brain and she couldn't keep quiet. "How can your enemies be so sure Hana is your child?"

Khal didn't speak for a moment, and then he reached inside his breast pocket and drew out a document. "They may have had sight of this. People talk…"

"What is it?" Beth said fearfully.

"It's the proof that Hana is my daughter."

"Proof?"

"Don't look at me like that, Beth. Our daughter is a royal princess. I had to be certain. And now we both know that Hana is a member of the royal house of Hassan—"

"And I'll never be allowed to forget it, will I?" Beth said, turning the official-looking envelope over in her hands. She didn't need to read it, she had guessed the contents.

"Why don't you open it?" Khal said.

She pulled out the single type-written sheet and paled as her worst fears were confirmed. "There is only way you could have got this, and that's by having someone come into the labour room while I was recovering from Hana's birth and take samples from her."

"It was a necessary precaution."

"You think that sending an intruder into a labour room is acceptable?"

"I deemed it necessary." He shrugged. "But there was no intruder, because that person was already there."

Beth gasped as the implication of Khal's cool statement hit home. *"Who?* Who did this, Khal?" Beth's eyes filled with tears as she thought back to her lonely vigil in a room full of strangers. She had been strong then for Hana's sake, but her sense of betrayal now was overwhelming. She was in such turmoil, it was a struggle to remember every face and name of the medical professionals who had been with her in the birthing room.

"Don't be so naïve, Beth," Khal said impatiently as she bit down on her fist to stop the tears. "As soon as I knew you were pregnant my team moved into action."

"Your *team?*" It was worse than she had thought. He hadn't even handled this personally. But then why would he, when the ruler of Q'Adar had someone to carry out even this most personal of all tasks for him?

"I didn't take any chances," Khal explained as if this were reasonable. "I ordered a daily report on your progress."

"From your spies?" Beth bit back.

"Do you imagine I would leave the birth of a baby that was almost certainly mine to chance?"

"Yes, Hana's your child, Khal," Beth reminded him, stung more than she could say by the fact that he thought there could have been doubt over Hana's parentage. "Your *child...*" She wondered if Khal had any understanding of what it meant to be a parent.

"I had a war to fight," he reminded her coldly, so distanced from her now they were like two strangers. It seemed to her that after a few moments of humanity Khal had slipped back into his old, hard ways.

You could have called me.

"Are you suggesting I should have given my position away, along with that of the men fighting with me? Isn't it enough to be separated from my child without having you lecture me on what I should have done, when I did all I could to keep you and the men in the desert with me safe?"

"But the way you went about it."

"Ensuring Hana was my child? This is a big thing, Beth. We're not talking about any ordinary child."

"No child is ordinary," she fired back at him.

He bowed his head in acknowledgement that this time she was right. "But all the same I had to be sure. And for your safety and my peace of mind, that was *my* doctor, *my* anaesthetist, *my* nurse, and *my* paediatric specialist with you when Hana was born. You should be thanking me instead of this. You surely didn't think I would turn my back on you when you were carrying my baby?"

"They could have told me." The subterfuge was getting to her. She accepted his explanation regarding the need for discretion, but Khal's calculating actions almost made her wish he *had* abandoned them. The fact that Hana was a royal child deserving of some special treatment made Beth feel like a convenient womb, and made Hana sound like nothing more than the result of a successful and very privileged breeding programme. "Stop…stop it," she begged him, covering her ears with her hands. "Don't say another word. I can't bear to hear you talking about Hana like this."

"Like what?"

"As if she wouldn't be so precious without royal blood running through her veins."

"Before you judge me, examine your own conscience. How long would you have waited before trying to contact me again?"

"The Q'Adaran embassy refused to give me your number." Before Beth had a chance to say any more, the limousine drew up outside the VIP entrance and, taking Hana from her arms, Khal got out of the limousine, leaving Beth to scramble after him.

Beth was stunned to find Faith waiting for them in the VIP lounge.

"You mentioned Hana's routine, and so I had your attendant brought here," Khal told her as he handed Hana over.

"Faith isn't my attendant, she's my friend. But, thank you…" She looked at him properly and saw the lines of tension on his face. She would forgive him his comment about Faith, because that was just a symptom of Khal's distance from her life. It was something that, if she stayed with him, she would have to change. But for now she was worried about him. "Is there somewhere we can sit down?" she said, extending an olive branch. For a moment she thought he would, or maybe he wanted to, but then he shook his head.

"When I've introduced Faith to members of my staff, and greeted all these dignitaries…"

She saw them then, lined up and waiting for him. However tired he was, and whatever the demands on him personally, Khal would always do his duty and do it well.

He was gone some time before he could join her in the private lounge. "Do you have everything you need?" he asked, swinging back into the room in a flurry of sandalwood and energy.

"Everything, thank you," Beth said, wishing they didn't have to be so stiff with each other. She patted the seat beside her and a after a moment's hesitation he joined her. "You asked me in the limousine why I didn't take action when Hana was born. I didn't want anything from you, Khal, and that was why. I just didn't see the point."

"You were entitled to my support," he said, turning his proud face towards her.

She was so relieved they were communicating again she didn't want to break the mood, and knew this wasn't the time to admit she had feared rattling the cage of Khal's formidable legal-team, and had buried her head in the sand to some extent. "I wouldn't have kept on working at Khalifa if I'd been trying to hide from you."

"Or maybe you had nowhere else to go," Khal suggested, getting up to pour them both a soft drink.

"I've got my family…"

He noticed how she flinched at the lie, and he flinched too, but inwardly. He didn't want this, but perhaps it was better if the truth came out. He knew more than Beth thought he did. His investigations hadn't concentrated solely on her pregnancy. "Why didn't you go to your family?" He turned to face her. "Why didn't they come to you, Beth?" He knew this was cruel, but it had to be said. He couldn't live with deception any more, he'd had enough of it in Q'Adar.

Seeing he knew the truth, she looked away. "Well?" he pressed. "Isn't it time you told me about your family, Beth? From what you've said about them I imagine they must have been thrilled to hear about the baby. No? Is that the reason you haven't gone near them while you were pregnant…or when you had the baby?"

Her blue eyes filled with tears, but still she raised them to meet his gaze. "You know about that too, don't you, Khal? You know all my talk on the beach was just that—talk. I don't have a family. Or at least I didn't have a family until Hana was born. I had the store, I had Khalifa; that was my family. And that's why my job means so much to me," she admitted huskily.

He remained silent. He'd known for some time that Beth's stories on the beach had just been her sad little daydreams, and now he had trampled them it didn't make him proud.

As always she rallied fast. "I might not have a family, and a fancy support-structure like you, but I can still appoint a lawyer to act for me, and—"

"And I will fight you," he assured her, instinct driving him. Launching a defence against every threat that came his way was bred into him.

"I expected that," she told him tensely. "I expect you to stop at nothing to get your own way, Khal."

"Don't you think Hana deserves to know both her parents? I want her to enjoy her birthright both as my daughter and as a princess of Q'Adar. Surely as her mother you would want that for her?"

"I want Hana to be happy, and that's all I care about."

"And I want that too."

"No, Khal, you want to take Hana from me and bring her up believing that money and power is everything, and love doesn't matter." Was he even listening? Beth wondered.

"If you fight me," he warned, "I'll apply for full custody. Are you prepared to lose Hana?"

"Don't threaten me." But just the thought of losing Hana was so terrible her voice was shaking, and all the bravado and cheerfulness that had always lifted her had gone. And for the first time in her life Beth felt beaten.

"All I want is my legal entitlement as Hana's father, a father who can provide the type of life Hana deserves."

"The life Hana deserves?" Beth repeated, shrinking inside.

"Try to understand that the difference in our circumstances dictates—"

"Dictates *what,* Khal? That with your fabulous wealth and immense power you can buy a lawyer, buy a judge, buy a child?"

"It isn't like that, Beth, and you know it. You're distraught."

"You bet I am!"

"Your choice is simple. You can stay in Liverpool and take your chances, or you can come to Q'Adar with me and Hana." He glanced towards the runway where his private jet was waiting. "Either way, Hana goes with me."

Put so starkly, Beth could only think about Hana's safety. In the final analysis it was the only thing that mattered to her. "Are you sure you can keep her safe?"

"Decision time, Beth…"

"I won't be your mistress."

"I'll make the necessary arrangements for you

to board the flight." Khal cut across her without emotion.

And that was it. She felt grief for what they'd lost, but this fast decision-making and brevity of speech fit the dangerous times through which Khal was living, and she knew she could expect nothing more. With Hana always first in her mind, she thanked him and said they would be ready to leave the moment they were called.

"Tell Hana's nanny that she will also be made welcome in Q'Adar." It wasn't much, but he wanted to give Beth something. It had never been his intention to crush her, or to have her return to Q'Adar under duress. As he held her gaze, something tugged at his heart, and instinctively he made the Q'Adaran gesture for a blessing that he had made so many times before to so many people, but never to the one person who needed it most.

While Beth went to see to Hana he sat heavily on a chair, staring through the panoramic windows, seeing nothing. He was still reeling from the shock of holding his baby daughter for the first time, and seeing Beth again. She challenged him every step of the way—but did he want the mother of his child to be a lioness or a milksop? He couldn't guarantee their safety in England, but Q'Adar would always be turbulent; it was the nature of the people. She would have to be strong, and deep down he knew she would cope, because Beth was an exceptional woman. She challenged everything he believed in—his views on life, and even his role in it. No one had ever done that before; no one had ever dared.

He'd always known she wasn't malleable mistress-material, but that didn't stop him wanting her in his life. If there was a solution to this, he couldn't see it. He couldn't marry Beth, and she would never agree to be his mistress. And so he must be content. Bringing Beth and Hana back with him to Q'Adar where he could keep them safe was the result he had aimed for when he'd come to England. He had succeeded in that, and it would have to be enough for him to know they were under his protection now.

He *was* content, Khal told himself...or as content as he ever could be.

CHAPTER ELEVEN

THE ruler of Q'Adar's preferred mode of transport wasn't a small private jet, but a full-sized airliner with the royal crest of a hawk emblazoned on its tail, and the royal standard flying from the nose of the plane. Beth was standing with Hana in her arms on the tarmac, and they were being escorted to the plane by security staff. This was how it would be from now on, Beth realised. Khal was still making his way down the line of dignitaries, and looked magnificent in his flowing Arabian robes.

"Where's Faith?" he asked the moment he could get away.

"She received a phone call to say her father has been taken ill. I took the liberty of asking your driver to take her home. I hope you don't mind?"

"You did the right thing," Khal told her, and then instead of sweeping in front of her he paused at the foot of the steps. "Shall I take Hana for you?"

It didn't take a flock of royal attendants hurrying to her side to tell Beth how incongruous this offer was. She couldn't imagine many sheikhs took their baby, the baby no one had previously known about, into their arms in full view of everyone. "I can manage, thank you," she said, staring up to where the flight attendants were waiting to greet them, in what was to all intents and purposes Q'Adar.

Aware of Khal close behind her, Beth mounted the steps with Hana in her arms. Behind Khal came a contingent of his office and security staff. She had to wonder what they made of their leader's ready-made family. To his credit Khal didn't seem in the least bit concerned.

"Would you like to put Hana in a cot?" he suggested as they entered a reception area on board the plane. "I've made sure there are several cots on board," he told Beth, when he saw the surprise on her face.

She held Hana a little more closely, feeling overwhelmed now she was here.

"I'll show you round so you know where everything is." She looked very small and very young, clutching her child close to her, but he could understand Beth's apprehension. She had made a brave decision, and could sense that she was in Q'Adaran territory now. He led the way into a comfortable lounge, as spacious as anything she might find in a luxury hotel, hoping to reassure her. "If you need anything, you only have to ask."

"Thank you," she said politely, with a face that was carefully expressionless.

"No one will disturb you, but if you require anything you only have to ring this bell."

Her eyes widened and then quickly became masked again. "If you show me where everything is, I can help myself..."

As she stopped speaking and looked at him, he saw she knew that he didn't know where anything was. He only had to ring a bell and whatever he wanted came to him. He had never had to go looking for a thing in his life. "The staff will do that for you," he said. "You don't want to insult them by refusing their help, do you?"

"That's different, then," she agreed as he tried not to notice her delicate perfume.

He showed her more rooms located off a long

and luxuriously carpeted corridor, conscious that this was the first time in his life he had ever acted as a tour guide. She started talking to Hana, explaining things to her, showing complete disregard for his instructions about holding conversations with a royal baby. "And just in case you need a doctor," he said, indicating another room, "this is the medical centre."

"I sincerely hope we won't need a doctor."

"And there are two bedrooms at this end of the plane, each with cots. Feel free to choose whichever you like. I have my own quarters at the front of the aircraft, so you won't disturb me."

"I wouldn't dream of it."

He continued on as if he hadn't heard her. "And my support staff will be at the rear of the plane in a completely different section, so they won't disturb you."

"That's reassuring, isn't it, Hana?"

"There are three bathrooms, all with a shower and whirlpool bath."

"And a good stock of towels?"

"Of course."

"Have you ever thought of going into real estate?" she said.

"And there's a cinema in here."

"No swimming pool?"

He stopped, and turned to face her.

"Do you have a cot for Hana in the lounge?" she said innocently. "Only I didn't see one."

"I'll have one brought in for you. And there's a professional nanny on board. I would have ordered two if I'd known Faith couldn't be here."

"You'd have *ordered* one?—like pizza?"

He looked down at her.

"Not like pizza, like people you value, Khal, because they're part of our team."

"*Our* team?"

She blushed. "I don't need a nanny, thank you very much. No offence to the nanny."

"And none taken...by the nanny."

He flew the plane too. Couldn't he delegate anything to other people? Beth wondered as Khal left her in a swirl of robes that cast up the scent of sandalwood and amber. That was how she would always think of him, Beth realised as her heart lurched, the rugged warrior sheikh with his darkly glittering glamour, and his dangerous, cold black eyes.

The flight was smooth and uneventful, and when the landing gear went down Beth was surprised to find she was excited by the prospect of returning to Q'Adar. Gazing out of the window, she realised things were starting to change for the better under Khal's rule. In the time she had been away, and even taking into account the uprising, he had managed to transform large tracts of desert into a garden of crops. She wanted to congratulate him, but when they landed and the plane drew to a halt on the tarmac she was disappointed to see a limousine waiting for her, while a smaller, faster car sped away with Khal at the wheel.

This was how it would be, Beth realised: the ruler of Q'Adar on a faster and more demanding track, while his illegitimate baby daughter and her mother slipped into the shadows behind tinted windows. But she couldn't help feeling a sense of anticipation at the thought of making things work out for the best for Hana in Q'Adar. At least until Khal told them it was safe to go home. She would never think of Q'Adar as home, would she? Beth reflected as the limousine slid past the soothing sight of orange groves, packed with ripe fruit glowing like tiny Halloween lanterns in the fast-fading sun.

Gunning the engine of his Ferrari until it threatened to take flight, Khal was still debating how exactly Beth was going to fit into court life in Q'Adar. Pure instinct had made him bring her here without any of his usual thought and planning, but when there was a threat to those he cared about he acted fast and decisively. He had never brought a woman to the palace before, and yet here he was with a ready-made family. He'd have to find something to keep Beth busy and out of his way...

"This is our life for now," Beth whispered to baby Hana as the limousine slowed in front of the grand entrance of the palace. She was taking comfort in the warm baby-scent, with her face buried in Hana's downy black curls, but when she saw the Dowager Sheikha waiting to greet them at the top of the steps her head snapped up. "Oh, great," Beth breathed with genuine pleasure, her face lighting with enthusiasm as she remembered how kind Khal's mother had been to her on her previous visit. All the plans Beth had been making on the way to the palace— To achieve any one of them she'd need an influential supporter.

Oh, great, Beth thought, biting her lip as she began to lose confidence. She couldn't imagine Khal's mother would feel much like playing fairy godmother when the clumsy shop-girl from the ball returned to the palace with a royal baby in her arms…

Beth's stomach was performing cartwheels by the time the Dowager Sheikha, minus her usual entourage, came purposefully down the steps. But the driver was opening the door, and there was nothing for it but to get out with Hana and face the music.

"Welcome to Q'Adar, my dear!"

Khal's mother swooped on them, enveloping Beth and Hana in a flurry of floating lavender fabric, delicious scent and tinkling jewellery. Was it possible she had changed so much the Dowager Sheikha didn't recognise her? Beth wondered. "Well, hello again." She dipped into a curtsey, fully expecting the bubble to have burst by the time she rose to her feet.

"No need for that, dear." The Dowager Sheikha

put her hand beneath Beth's elbow to support her as she rose again, and her perfume made Hana sneeze. "Oh, she's adorable! May I hold her?"

"Of course..." Beth was still trying to accustom herself to the warmth of her welcome.

"This is what we need in Q'Adar," Khal's mother confided as they walked up the steps together.

"What's that, Your Majesty?"

"Young blood," the Dowager Sheikha insisted. She paused at the top of the steps to give Beth a quick once-over.

And how did she rate? Beth wondered, thinking back to all the glamorous princesses Khal's mother had assembled at the ball for her son's approval. It was hard to tell what the older woman was thinking behind those penetrating, raisin-black eyes.

"Shall I hand Hana over to the nurses for you? My son has engaged an army of support staff."

Beth recoiled. "No."

"No?"

The last thing she wanted now was a disagreement with the nicest of women, but, like her son, the Dowager Sheikha wasn't used to hearing the word "no", unless it came from her own mouth. "No." Beth spoke more gently this time. "Hana won't be needing an army of support staff, but what she does need is rest after such a long journey. We're not used to being separated, you see—"

"Not even at the store?" the Dowager Sheikha interrupted. "I understood that when you're working Hana is in the crèche?"

Exactly how much had Khal told his mother? Beth wondered. "I'm on hand all the time, and a very good friend of mine—a school friend who lives with us—works at the crèche and is with Hana every moment."

"I see." Khal's mother considered this. "You seem to have it all under control."

Beth kept her thoughts on that to herself.

"I admire you, Beth Torrance."

"You do?"

"Yes."

Touching Beth's cheek, the Dowager Sheikha smiled at her, and for the first time since leaving England Beth felt a little glow of confidence blossom inside her. Maybe she would achieve a few of the small things she hoped to, things she believed she could offer Q'Adar in the short time she would be have. With Khal's mother on-side, the future didn't seem so bleak. But she would never get used to this, Beth thought, as servants bowed and doors opened in front of them as if by magic.

"I chose the garden suite for you myself," the Dowager Sheikha informed Beth, drawing to a halt in front of a pair of exquisite gold-filigree doors. "I think this apartment enjoys one of the most beautiful aspects in the palace, plus the courtyard and gardens have plenty of shade for baby Hana." She stared longingly at Hana, asleep in Beth's arms. "When she wakes—"

"I'll see that you're informed immediately."

"Oh, would you?" Khal's mother turned grateful eyes on her. "It's been a long time since we've had a baby at the palace, and I'd like to read to her, and maybe sing to her a little…"

And what would Khal make of that? Beth wondered. Would he dare to disapprove? Her eyes twinkled at the thought of this double-pronged rebellion by the women in his life.

Any thoughts Beth might have harboured about being stuffed away in an attic somewhere out of sight were immediately obliterated when she walked into the cool tiled hallway of her new home. "It's next door to my own apartment," the Dowager Sheikha told her as she bustled ahead. "I planned it this way, hoping I might catch glimpses of baby Hana in the garden…"

As she turned, Beth saw the same longing in her eyes again. "You can sit with Hana, or push her round the courtyard, any time you want." Did dowager sheikhas do things like that?

"I'd love to!" Khal's mother exclaimed, dispelling Beth's fears.

Judging by that response, Beth guessed Khal's mother was pretty much like herself and didn't mind starting new trends when she had to.

"I'm going to leave you now, and give you chance to settle in," she said. "I expect you'd like a little time to get used to your new surroundings."

She would never get used to them, Beth thought, acting like a tourist already, turning circles to stare up at the gloriously ornate painted ceiling.

"You'll have your own household, of course," Khal's mother added at the door.

"My own household?" Beth repeated incredulously. "Why would I need that?"

"Enjoy your temporary status as a member of
the royal family," the Dowager Sheikha insisted
with a mischievous twinkle.

"You're very generous, Your Majesty," Beth
said, remembering her manners as she bobbed a
curtsey. "But it really isn't necessary."

"Nonsense, you'll enjoy it. And I shall make
the introductions myself," Khal's mother decided
on impulse, beckoning to the staff hovering outside. "It's better if you don't confide too many
details," she murmured confidentially, returning
to Beth's side.

Beth's eyes widened as she gazed down the
line of neatly uniformed staff. "But, if all these
people are going to be looking after Hana and
me, surely they deserve to know the situation?"

"You have a lot to learn, my dear."

"Don't we all?" Beth sighed. Then, quickly remembering herself, she added, "Well, obviously
not you, Your Majesty."

CHAPTER TWELVE

HE was on his way to the stables when he saw his mother hurrying towards him.

"The baby's adorable!" she exclaimed, clasping her hands together in delight. "And I've seen your little friend settled in as you requested." As he turned to go, she put her hand on his arm. "Won't you stay a little while and talk with me, Khalifa?"

"I'm not in the mood to talk, and Beth is not 'my little friend'. Hana's mother is called Beth Tracey Torrance."

"But I may call her Beth on your instruction, is that it, Khal? Too kind…"

"Sarcasm doesn't suit you, Mother."

"And neither does this aloof manner suit you, Khalifa. And I hope you're not thinking of riding out without guards."

"There's a storm brewing, enough to keep the troublemakers in their burrows. Don't be concerned about me," he added, seeing his mother's concern. "I can read the desert."

"Can you, Khalifa?"

He looked at his mother's hand on his sleeve, saw the tension in her face, and knew she was remembering. "I must have some freedom." As her hand relaxed, he firmed his resolve and bowed to her. "If you will excuse me..."

"You won't find an answer to your Beth in the desert."

"She is not *my* Beth, and I am trialling a horse," he said with as much restraint as he could muster.

"Whatever you say. Be careful, my son."

As Beth had suspected Hana wanted nothing more than to sleep after her long journey. The facilities in the nursery were incredible, and the girls on duty were graduates of a college that had been at the forefront of childcare training for over a hundred years. After chatting with them, Beth felt confident enough to leave Hana in their care and take a look around.

The Palace of the Moon was on such a mammoth scale it took Beth a few minutes to reach her private garden. She hadn't been invited to visit this more secluded and very special part of the palace on her last visit to Q'Adar, so when she entered through a gate she gave an exclamation of delighted surprise. It was just like finding the secret garden, she thought, remembering one of her favourite childhood books. The stone walls held the scent of the flowers, intensifying it, and there were colonnades around the perimeter which offered shade along narrow pathways. The sultry temperature of late afternoon was made bearable thanks to the central fountain, which cast plumes of twinkling water high into the air. Having showered and changed in her fabulous bathroom, Beth was wearing a pair of loose-fitting lightweight trousers and a shirt, and felt refreshed, but it was still tempting to perch on the raised lip of the pool and throw her head back to catch the spray.

Dressed for riding in breeches and a shirt, he watched her from the shadows. A new stallion awaited him, the finest of his kind. It was a gift from a neighbouring sheikh, and under normal circumstances nothing could have delayed his inspection. The horse had recently knocked a couple of seconds off the fastest recorded time on a measured track, and he had yet to try him out. That should have been enough to blank everything else from his mind, but it appeared Beth was an exception, and his senses roared as she turned her face to the sky and sighed with pleasure. There was one answer, and that was exercise—fierce and hard.

"Khal…?"

He paused mid-stride. Had she sensed his presence? She certainly hadn't seen him, and he was moving away from her on silent feet. Was it possible they were so finely tuned that she'd known all along he had been watching her? He stepped out of the shadows and strode across the courtyard. "I trust your quarters are acceptable?"

"My quarters? If you mean my fabulous apartment, it's great!"

He had to stop himself smiling. How could he have forgotten the effect she always had on him? "Great?" he said dryly, thinking of the kings and presidents who had stayed there before her. "Well, as long as you're satisfied and have everything you need."

"Oh, I do," she assured him, turning her attention

to some rose petals floating on the pond. "Does someone toss these into the water each day?"

"Why? Would you like the job?"

She looked at him, and he saw the surprise in her eyes at the flash of humour. He agreed with her, it was ill-judged. Beth was here because he wanted to keep her and Hana safe. The last thing he wanted was to remind them both of times when they had been intimate, both in bed and out of it.

"I'd like *a* job, Khal," she said, rushing to paper over the cracks as he had done. "Though I doubt I'll be here long enough. But I do have an idea."

Why wasn't he surprised? "Go on..."

"Well, you don't have a palace crèche, do you?"

"There's only one royal baby, as far as I am aware," he pointed out.

"But there must be dozens more amongst the staff, and you obviously have contact with one of the greatest nursery-nurse colleges in the world. It just seemed to me..."

"Yes?" he pressed, eager to escape so he would no longer have to look into those crystal-blue eyes.

"Well, I just thought you could throw it open."

"To all-comers?" He frowned.

"To everyone employed at the palace. It will be company for Hana, and I'm happy to help out. I could even run it for you."

"You won't be here that long." He could have kicked himself when her face fell.

"No, I forgot."

She tipped up her chin. She had been carried away by a scheme she had no hope of seeing through, and in doing so believed she had made a fool of herself.

"It was just a thought," she said, frowning.

"I'm expecting to hear that the danger has passed very soon and that you'll be able to go home."

"Oh, good…"

Did her voice sound a little flat, or was he imagining it?

"This is nice for Hana." She glanced around the elegant courtyard. "But I wouldn't want her getting used to it."

He rapped his whip across his riding boots. When he had worked out the next stage of Hana's integration into royal life, he'd let Beth know. Meanwhile, why shouldn't she enjoy the palace and all it had to offer? "If you like riding I'll ask my groom to find you a horse so you can ride around the palace grounds."

"Would you?"

As her eyes lit with enthusiasm, he realised Beth had mistaken this for an invitation, but what he had planned for himself was something more rigorous. "Yes, I'll do that while I'm down there," he said, giving his thighs a tap with the crop. "I'll tell them to sort something out for you."

"But aren't you riding in the grounds?"

"I have other plans. A groom will ride with you, if you like, show you around."

"That won't be necessary, thank you," she told him. Her eyes were wounded, though she tilted her chin in the usual way.

"Well, I'd better get on," he said. "I want to make the most of the daylight." With considerable relief, he strode away.

The palace stables—why not? Even if Khal didn't want to ride with her, riding here would be a real adventure. Not that she'd go far, of course. She'd keep to the gardens as Khal had suggested.

Beth checked on Hana before she left, and was

pleased to find her suggestions had been carried out to the letter. Hana was still sleeping contentedly, with the two nurses in attendance. Down in the stables, she discovered that Khal hadn't let her down. The pony they brought out for her approval was a sweet grey with a kind face, just the type of horse to give a novice confidence.

She was still wearing trousers and a shirt, and they lent her some boots with a heel to stop her foot slipping out of the stirrup, and also a freshly laundered bandana to keep the dust from her face. The grooms echoed Khal's words, telling her she must stay within the palace grounds. She was fine with that. They palace grounds were like a vast park, with plenty of opportunity to give the small pony his head.

But when she rode past one of the archways and saw the desert rolling back as far as she could see, the lure proved too much for her. She couldn't imagine any remaining insurgents would dare to come within sight of the palace. Ducking her head as she passed beneath the stone arch, she gave the guard a confident greeting as if this had all been arranged. He grew alert, as if to challenge her, but then thought better of it when she squeezed her knees to give her pony the signal to trot. She would just ride once round the palace and then return, Beth decided.

The pony responded eagerly to the promise of the desert. He carried her at a brisk pace beyond the walls, onto a shadowy carpet of sand beneath a moon in a tangerine-and-lilac sky. She rode out a bit further, and then a little further still. She felt safe as long as she could still see the palace. She was on the point of urging the pony into a controlled canter when she first caught sight of Khal in silhouette against the darkening sky. So he hadn't planned to ride in the grounds, after all. He was galloping as fast as she had seen any man ride, and his horse was stretched out like an arrow with its tail flying behind like a silken banner in the wind.

She could have sat there and watched them for hours, it was such a romantic sight. He was heading for a small fort, she noticed. What was the attraction? Beth wondered, turning her horse and trotting after him. It looked as though the crumbling building had been unoccupied for years. It was little more than an old ruin, with a yawning gap where once there must have been grand gates, and gaping holes instead of windows. It must be another one of Khal's projects, Beth guessed, squeezing her knees to give her pony the signal to move faster. She wanted to keep within range so she could admire Khal's skill on horseback. He really was amazing...

Beth tensed, hearing a sound like rolling thunder coming up behind her. Her heart fluttered an alarm as she reined in and turned in the saddle. It took her a moment to process the information, it was so surreal. It seemed that a wall of sand reaching high into the sky was sweeping towards her. And Khal wasn't simply testing his horse, Beth realised, he was riding for his life! As she must, if Hana wasn't to lose both her parents in one catastrophic incident.

She had never galloped flat-out, but now she must, it was that or become swallowed up by the sand. Pressing the little pony as hard as she could, Beth leaned forward in the saddle, gripping hanks of mane to keep her safe. Ramming her heels down in the stirrups, she prayed she wouldn't fall off. It was hard to see where she was going as the driving dust began to catch up with her. And then she saw a shadow, and realised

Khal had spotted her and turned round. He was going to cross her path. He was coming for her, coming to save her, Beth realised, sobbing with relief. He was waving a warning, and pointing to the shelter of the fort. It was little enough protection, but she could see it was the only hope they had. To turn for the palace meant turning into the path of the storm. Thoughts of Hana drove Beth forward. Her baby couldn't lose both her parents!

The pony strained beneath her, moving as fast as it could, with its ears back and its eyes wild, as aware as she was that this was one race it couldn't afford to lose. "Don't fall off!" Beth chanted to herself grimly as the sand scoured her skin and clouded her eyes, making them water. But as the roaring grew steadily louder Beth began to realize there was no hope.

But now Khal had cut across her path, and was galloping alongside her. "Lose your stirrups!"

Take her feet out of the stirrups? Was he mad? She'd fall off! "Leave me! Save yourself! I'll catch up." They both knew that would never happen. But she didn't stand a chance, so at least one of them could be saved.

"Do it!" he snapped. Leaning across at full gallop, he caught hold of her reins and brought their two horses closer.

Her teeth were juddering in her jaw as she risked a glance. Khal wasn't going anywhere unless she went with him. He wasn't even going to try to save himself. She freed her feet, her scream of terror lost in a thunder of hooves as Khal grabbed her firmly round the waist. He yanked her into his arms. His horse sprang forward competitively as Beth's mount raced ahead, freed of the weight on its back, while Beth clung to Khal in a state of shock and pure relief.

He held her tight and safe in front of him as the stallion galloped for the fort. They were muscle to muscle, flesh to flesh, as he called out and thrashed the reins from side to side on its neck to urge the stallion on. Beth wasn't even sure she breathed again until they raced beneath the archway into a maze of ancient buildings, but the wall of sand followed them even there, blowing them deeper into the crumbling sanctuary. Khal dragged Beth with him as he dismounted, and her pony blundered blindly in after them. Capturing his reins as well as the stallion's, Khal led both horses as well as Beth to the shelter of a wall where perhaps they stood a chance.

"You saved my life!" Beth gasped, pressing back against the stone in an attempt to keep upright as the storm rushed over them.

"Not yet!" Khal rasped grimly, shielding her with his body, arms planted either side of her face as he yelled at her. "What were you doing out here in the desert on your own? Don't you know how dangerous it is?"

No, she didn't, and the fierce expression on Khal's face told Beth he was thinking of another time, and another far more dreadful incident than this, an incident that had ripped out his heart. "I'm sorry."

"Sorry? You could have been killed."

"Khal, please, I know I shouldn't have—"

"You know nothing," he cut across her fiercely, and then his face contorted, and as she reached out to him he pulled away. "Life is precious."

"Forgive me." But Khal wasn't interested in her compassion now, and shook her off.

"We just have to hope we get lucky and the storm veers away," he told her grimly.

Subject closed. How she wished she could find

something to say to touch the pain inside him and ease it somehow.

And the storm didn't veer away. Instead the sand and dust continued to pour into their ruined sanctuary. "Here," Khal said, ripping the bandana from his neck. "Cover your pony's eyes." Tearing off his shirt, he wrapped it around his stallion's head. Then, dragging Beth to him, he kept his arm over her head as she buried her face in his chest.

"You saved my life," she whispered unheard against Khal's hard, unyielding flesh. She couldn't believe he'd done this for her; she couldn't believe they had survived. All she wanted to do now was thank him, heal him, save him... "Khal, speak to me," she begged him when the noise of the storm had abated a little.

"About what?" But, when he saw she knew and understood, and that it was no use hiding the facts from her any longer, he grated out, "I lost her here in the desert."

"Who did you lose?" Beth probed gently.

"My sister, Ghayda. I lost her to the quicksand. I couldn't save her..."

"Oh, Khal, I'm so sorry..." It explained so much

about him. And it also told Beth that, though she loved Khal as much as she did, it wasn't enough, and that she must help him lose this heavy burden of guilt or he would never be capable of feeling again. Forgetting how he'd shrugged her off, she put her arms around him and held him, not in lust but with love and compassion, as the wind roared around them.

They seemed to stand there for hours until Khal informed her that, as he'd hoped, the storm had swung away. So it had, Beth realised with surprise as Khal eased free of her embrace. She had been so swept up in a different storm, a storm of their own making, that she hadn't even noticed. But now she felt like celebrating, because, for all the tons of sand that had poured in through the gaps in the stonework, half-burying them, they were alive, *they had made it through together!*

Beth's first thought was for Hana. "Will they know what's happened to us at the palace?"

"You can ring them." Khal pulled out a phone and handed it to her. "When you're finished, I must speak to my aide-de-camp."

Beth stared at the small mobile-phone. It seemed impossible there could still be communication with the outside world after all that had happened.

"Is Hana all right?" Khal asked the moment Beth ended the call.

"She's fine, sleeping soundly."

It was so strange to have someone who cared as much about Hana as she did, Beth thought, as Khal delivered his information in brisk, no-nonsense Arabic. Right now she was proud to call him the father of her child. And then, perhaps because all her emotions had been stretched and tested to the limit, the most inappropriate emotion of all surfaced.

"What?" Khal said, frowning at her as he stowed the phone in his breeches.

"Do I look like you?" Beth had to press her lips down very hard to stop herself giggling, because her tall, dark, handsome sheikh had been transformed by the dust of the desert into a snowman. His thick, wavy black hair was fully coated, and his face was white too.

Khal retaliated with a scorching survey of his own. "I don't know about me, but you could do with a wash," he said dryly.

"Some hope of that!"

"You'd be surprised," he said, with a slight tug of his lips that made her heart turn over.

"I certainly would," she agreed, determined to appear cool.

"Come with me if you don't believe me."

As Beth stared at Khal's outstretched hand, her humour gave way to emotion. "You saved my life," she whispered again huskily.

"And you've got guts." His eyes shot fire into her heart, and then he laughed. "And you look like a chimney sweep."

And you look gorgeous even now, Beth thought. "You don't think I'm going to go anywhere with you, do you?" she teased him. "You could be anyone under that desert-sand face mask."

"Could we market them at the stores, do you think?" he said, pretending to think about it. "It's the best exfoliation I've ever had."

Did he have to thumb the stubble on his jaw like that? "A speciality line, maybe?" Beth suggested, enjoying the joke

"That's something we can talk about later."

"Later?" She loved the sound of that word.

"But right now," he said, reaching for her hand, "It's bath time…"

"You were serious!" Beth exclaimed in astonishment as she stared at the small lagoon.

"You've never heard of an oasis in the desert?"

"Of course I have." But this was beautiful, and she'd always thought the pictures she'd seen before must have been doctored to make things look more appealing. She couldn't imagine such lushness existed in the midst of such sun-parched nothingness. But the best thing of all was that she hadn't seen Khal so relaxed for a long time. "Snatching your life from the jaws of death" syndrome, perhaps. But didn't both of them have every right to feel on top of the world? "Engines?" Beth frowned, unwilling to believe anyone or anything would dare trespass upon their solitude.

"Helicopters," Khal confirmed. "Now they know where I am, there will be guards, guns... But don't worry—all my personal staff are trained to use the utmost discretion," he added, seeing Beth's concern.

"And that's just another price you have to pay?"

He shrugged. "I owe it to my people to stay alive."

The dangers were all around him. It made her

want to affirm the difference between living and life with him with everything she'd got.

He took pleasure in her wonder at their surroundings, and at the same time he was filled with an enormous sense of relief and happiness. The fact that they were alive, the fact that they were together, was all that mattered to him. The past and their disagreements seemed insignificant in the light of what they'd just been through. Going through it together and coming out safely the other side had to mean something. And it did. He hadn't realised just how much Beth Tracey Torrance meant to him until losing her had become a real possibility.

"This is the Pearl Oasis of Q'Adar," he murmured, hardly liking to intrude on her rapt contemplation of the scene. With her chin raised, and her face in profile with the breeze fluffing out her hair, she looked so beautiful.

"The Pearl Oasis of Q'Adar," she repeated, turning slowly to face him.

"Named for the lady Moon, who chooses to bathe here more frequently than in any other pool in the whole of Arabia."

"And I don't blame her!" Beth told him, with her eyes full of light. "It's so beautiful..."

He followed her gaze, to watch the crescent lantern glowing in the sky with its sprinkling of stars in attendance, and thought Beth twice as lovely. Below the moon the jagged peaks of the mountains cut sharply into the velvet sky, and lower still the oasis rippled lazily, so that the long streaks of milky moonlight reflected in its waters appeared to dance. Easing his neck, he exhaled with contentment. Standing here with Beth made him feel reborn. She made him see how beautiful this land, his kingdom, was, and how full of possibility it could be. He could forget the battles and think of a peaceful future with Beth at his side.

Beth stood in silence, drinking it in in case she never came here again. It was beyond beauty, beyond her experience, and reinforced what she already knew: that the majesty of nature far outweighed that of man. Time passed in solemn step between them, as they stood without word or explanation, and Beth felt they were growing closer all the time, floating in another world—the world of their thoughts, where possibilities were endless if you only had the courage to reach out and make them fact. She could have stayed happily all night, dreaming, but once again reality intruded and she became aware of scratchy sand in all manner of tender places. "Do you think my clothes will dry if I take them off and rinse them?" she said, turning to Khal.

"By morning they should."

"But doesn't it get cold in the desert at night?" Beth said, frowning.

"Not necessarily…"

CHAPTER THIRTEEN

KHAL built a big, warm fire and they set up camp around it. Their next job was to bathe the horses" eyes and make them comfortable, which Khal suggested they could do in the oasis.

"Do you mean take them swimming?"

"It's the best way to clean away all the dust and grit," he said. "What are you doing?"

Beth jumped as Khal turned from checking his horse's legs to stare at her. She had just been peering down the front of her shirt to see if her underwear would pass muster. Pulling her hand out, she laughed self-consciously. Khal had been half-naked for some time now. "It's all right for a man," she said. "But how can I strip off?" The moment she spoke, Beth wished she hadn't. The look Khal gave her cracked the dust on his cheek. He was right. Wasn't it a bit late for false modesty?

"Please yourself," he said, easing his powerful shoulders in a shrug. "But I'm going swimming."

And Beth had to admit the oasis did look tempting. She took a step back as Khal reached out. "Your face looks sore," he said, lowering his hand without touching her. "The water will clean the dust away. It's what you need."

Beth didn't answer. She only had to watch Khal's muscles flex as he checked his stallion over to know what she needed, and it was more than a wash.

Having removed the last of the horses" tack, Khal clicked his tongue against the roof of his mouth and they followed him to the lip of the lagoon. "I can't manage both of them," he said. "You'll have to come and help me…"

Beth watched transfixed as he unfastened his breeches and took them off. His black finest-cotton pants followed…

"You must have sand everywhere," he said, turning to face her.

No wonder he had no inhibitions, Beth thought. Even in the shadowy moonlight Khal's body was magnificent, a supreme work of nature, only exceeded by his supreme lack of self-consciousness as he sprang effortlessly onto his stallion's back. "What are you waiting for?" he said, turning to look at her over his shoulder.

For the fire to die down inside her, maybe? Though hopefully the cool water should accomplish that! Beth thought, waiting until the stallion had swum out a way. She had no idea why, when they had a child together, she should feel so self-conscious about the prospect of skinny-dipping with Khal. It was as if they were only now getting to know each other. She took her clothes off as quickly as she could, and, using the slope of the bank to her advantage, climbed up easily onto her pony's back. Squeezing her knees, she urged it into the water.

This was like something out of a film, Beth thought, as the warm breeze caressed her and the moon shone down on them. She rocked gently with surge of the pony's paddling motion, heading out towards Khal. He was right; after a grit bath this was just what she needed…he was just what she needed. And, judging by the angle of their horses" pricked ears, they thought so too.

She looked like a moon goddess coming towards him. The light was a strange mix of silver and some phosphorescent trickery conjured up by the light and the lingering heat. It gave her an aura that shimmered on her naked skin as her horse stepped out, and their mounts snickered companionably as she smiled at him.

He had been standing waiting for her, with the stallion fetlock-deep just off the shore beneath the shelter of some trees, wondering if he had ever felt so relaxed. When she reached him their mounts turned lazily towards a patch of grass that had survived the blistering heat of day beneath its canopy of leaves. Sound was contained by the mountains, and the swish of water as their horses moved through it seemed amplified, as did the hoot and scrabble of creatures of the night they couldn't see. The fantasy that they were alone in the world expanded and held firm for him. Beth's modesty was protected by her long blonde hair, which had curled damply around her nipples, allowing him no more than a tantalising glimpse of her breasts. She made no attempt to hide them, and as usual her chin was tipped at a confident angle. Anything she did she did wholeheartedly, and the way she had recovered after the storm had only increased his admiration for her.

"We can safely leave them to crop the grass," he said, dismounting from his horse. He came to help Beth down, and then the spell broke when she looked at him, because they both knew what would happen if she came into his arms.

"Why don't we swim?" she said, pulling back.

It hurt him more to see her innocent enthusiasm change to apprehension. The depth of her hurt and uncertainty about her future in Q'Adar was reflected in her face. In all honesty there was nothing he could say to reassure her—but he had saved her once, and now he wanted to save her again, and if that meant spending time with her… "Do you mean you want to go back in and swim without the horses?"

"That's exactly what I mean," she said, staring past him. "I've dreamed of swimming in the moonlight all my life, and I never thought I'd get the chance."

"Then tonight you will." Desire blazed inside him as he reached up for her. He could think of nothing but making her smile and relax again. He kept a safe distance between them as he lifted her down. "Before we swim I'm going to stoke the fire, so it will blaze all night and dry your clothes."

"I'll help you collect firewood," she offered.

"Brushwood, dried grass, twigs, anything you can find..." The desert wasn't generous with her scraps.

When that was done, she stood with her hand on her hips, watching him. "You make a mean fire, Sheikh..."

Enjoying the fact that she was relaxed now, he turned and gave her a mock bow. Then he saw her cheeks were blazing. They had been riding and walking in shadows, with the darkness concealing their nakedness, but like Eve she was aware of it now, and like Eve she wanted to run and hide and cover herself. He didn't want that for Beth. He didn't want her to feel ashamed, ever. It was important to him that she retained both her innocence and her pride. Reaching out, he took her hand to give her confidence, and just linking hands with her filled him with an emotion he'd never known before. They both knew this couldn't go anywhere, but while they had these few hours together why shouldn't they steal what pleasure they could?

Swimming with Khal in the moonlight was amazing. He was a much stronger swimmer than she was, but each time he overtook her he lay floating on his back, waiting for her to catch up as she thrashed energetically in the freestyle she'd learned at school.

"That was absolutely brilliant!" Beth exclaimed, finding her feet in the shallow water. But as the stones shifted she lost her balance and, lurching forward, grabbed on to Khal. He steadied her before letting go. "It must be boring for you having to swim with me."

"Why?" he said, lips curving into his delicious smile.

Beth changed tack rapidly. "I've never seen a moon so bright, have you?"

"Or so many stars…" Raking his hands through his hair to move it from his face, Khal leaned back into the water, floating, and Beth thought she had never seen him so relaxed. She was relaxed too, lost in the moment, thinking about the real man: the man in front of her now, the man who had previously been concealed beneath a cloak of power. When he stood she absorbed the stillness between them. She was aching for him to kiss her, and so she did the right thing and quickly moved away.

"Now, what are we going to do?" she said, adopting a perky voice. What indeed? How to retire with her self-respect intact when she was naked? "You'd better get out first, and I won't look," she suggested.

"Or we could stay here a little longer," Khal argued.

"And get cold?" Beth countered.

Khal's smile was so rare and so wicked, it made Beth doubt her self-control. "All right, I suppose I could warm you with my wit." The ironic expression on his face suggested not. "Or you should just turn your back and let me get out?"

"I prefer the first option."

"You do?"

"You offered to warm me," Khal reminded her, slicking water off his arms.

"I did?"

"Well?" he prompted. "I'm still waiting."

The moment of decision had come; she couldn't

keep on ducking and diving all night, and the moment she lifted her arms towards him she was lost. The hunger inside them both had been suppressed for far too long, and as Khal dragged her to him her inhibitions fell away. "Hold me close," she begged him; it was she who needed warming.

"Closer than this isn't possible."

"Yes, it is. You know it is," Beth argued.

He did know that. Swinging her into his arms, he carried her into the deeper water where he could stand and she could not. It hardly mattered, since her legs were already locked around his waist. "You've got me," he murmured against her mouth.

"You'd better believe it," she told him.

With Beth safe in one arm, he cupped her face with his hand and kissed her. She tasted like the missing part of him, and felt like it too. He hadn't realised how much he'd missed her, and he knew she must feel the same, because her feelings came pouring out in tears that he kissed away.

How could they ever get enough of each other? Even the chill of the water couldn't cool them now. She opened for him like a flower, leaning back as he eased into her, calling his name as her fingers bit into him, exhaling raggedly, eyes closed, giving herself up to pleasure.

Beth had blossomed into a woman since having the baby. She even tasted different, sweet and ripe and wonderful; everything about her was wonderful. She was hot for him, hot and wet, and her muscles gripped him with remorseless intent as he thrust deeper, taking her again and again, timing each thrust to the ebb of her sighs. He wanted nothing more than to give her pleasure. It was all that mattered to him. He wanted to watch her face and hear her moans of ecstasy, he wanted to serve her and see her dissolve into sensation; he wanted to make love to her until nothing existed for them outside of this...

"Oh, Khal, I can't hold back."

"You don't have to." The words had barely left his mouth before she bucked beneath him, and the sounds pouring from her lips became unfocused, unthinking and free. Free, as he longed to be.

When the storm of their love-making subsided, Khal carried her safely to the shore. "Do you feel warm now?" Beth teased him.

"Do you?"

"I do now," she purred as he joined her on their makeshift bed of grass.

"Then my job's done."

As he made to pull away she drew him back. "I see you still have the bad habit of teasing me." She stopped, not wanting to refer back to any time that hadn't been as happy as this. It was as if they had ventured into a magic kingdom, and she wasn't ready for reality yet. "Your Majesty," she said, lying back to tempt him on.

"Khal," he said, pausing for a kiss.

And even that wasn't something she could joke about. Khal's title and his position in the world carried too much weight. And that weight was all on his shoulders. "Khal," she amended softly, tracing the line of his hard, scarred mouth with her fingertip.

"That's better," he said, capturing her finger and warming it in his mouth.

He drew her into his arms and made love to her slowly this time, drawing out the pleasure until it couldn't be contained. In the water they had come together like two elemental beings who knew only a primitive urge to mate, but he wanted this to be different for Beth, and for him. Maybe he wanted something to remember her by, Khal reflected, something to keep him warm, and remind him what innocence could taste like after his inevitable return to the real world. He soothed her down, and then kissed her until she told him that she couldn't wait and that her whole body ached for him again. He refused to rush and kissed his way down her body until he reached her feet, and then he massaged them until she was purring like a kitten. He turned her then to drop kisses on the backs of her knees, which made her squirm and laugh.

"I had no idea…" Her words disintegrated.

"No idea?" He was moving on to feather kisses on her pale, silky thighs.

"That my legs could be so sensitive."

"You have so much to learn."

"And will you teach me?"

"For as long as you are here in Q'Adar." He felt her tense. It broke the mood. The length of time they'd have together was something neither one of them could predict.

"I want you so much." *And not just sexually*, though she must never tell Khal that. "I can't believe this night must end…" They lay together side by side, gazing at the stars.

"The night doesn't end until the fire goes out," Khal murmured.

"And as you've just put wood on it…" Turning on her stomach, Beth found her cheeky smile. "It's so special out here in the desert, isn't it?"

"I think so."

"I thought I'd hate it. I thought it would be barren, and cruel and hard."

"It is barren and cruel and hard."

"But it's beautiful too." She turned to him after a few more stolen minutes. "We should be getting back for Hana."

"I won't break my promise," Khal said. Reaching for her hand, he pressed the palm to his lips. "You'll be back before Hana wakes…"

She tried not to say anything, but as they stared at each other she couldn't hold the words back. "And then?"

"And then life carries on as before."

Beth's heart sank, and Khal telling her not to look so sad didn't help. She shouldn't be greedy; they'd had this night, this one magical night…

"Let's go and get the horses saddled up," Khal

suggested, springing to his feet. "Our clothes are dry," he confirmed, checking them out.

Reality had intruded, Beth realised, and now the dream was fading fast. There would be no more kisses and no more lingering looks as they tacked up the horses, ready to go. This was it.

Khal gave her a leg up and asked her if she felt safe before springing onto the back of his stallion.

Safe...

"Let's enjoy the ride back," he said, sensing her dejection. They should make the most of it, because he had nothing else to offer her—and though that left him feeling deeply unsatisfied it didn't mean they couldn't enjoy every moment they had left.

CHAPTER FOURTEEN

HE stood outside Hana's room the next morning, watching Beth nurse their baby. They had spent the night apart, and coming here to see them both had filled him with emotion. And yet he felt shut out too. It was the loss of all the months when he hadn't been there for them. But there was a better understanding between them now, and no reason why he shouldn't raise the subject of Beth staying on as his mistress. She had mellowed since having Hana, and he was more sensitive to her needs. His timing had been clumsy before, but this time, when he showed Beth the benefits of remaining in Q'Adar under his protection, he felt sure that she would see sense.

In spite of all the uncertainty, Beth was touched by the expression in Khal's eyes when she tiptoed out of Hana's room. There was such longing in them, as well as a softness she hadn't seen before. "Were you spying on me?"

"I was admiring your parenting skills," Khal admitted, falling into step with her. "Hana's so contented, and that's all thanks to you, Beth. You're a wonderful mother."

"Thank you..." Beth felt a little glow of pride and love for him, and, without suspecting anything, accepted Khal's suggestion that they have a refreshing drink together.

"I've been thinking about our future," he said, showing her into a shaded courtyard.

A fountain was tossing cooling plumes of rainbow spray into the air, and all around her there was something beautiful for Beth's glance to light on. She wondered if she had ever felt happier.

"It needn't be like this." Khal's look burned into her eyes.

But it was inevitable that it would be like this, Beth thought dreamily. When you loved as much as she did, how else could it be? The world glittered with a new light; it was a better place, and everything in it jumped into clear focus when you were in love.

"I don't like to see you upset," Khal said, drawing her out of the sun. "I don't like to hear you talking about lawyers—and most of all," he confessed, "I don't like to hear myself laying down the law where you're concerned."

"Are you telling me you're a reformed character?" Beth teased, feeling the glow of love she felt for Khal burst into flame. She felt like laughing for joy, and racing round the courtyard, spinning as she went in an effort to express the excitement and happiness inside her. She managed somehow to restrain herself and continue teasing him instead. "So you came round to my way of thinking in the end?"

"I can't say," Khal admitted, "As I don't know what you were thinking." He held Beth's gaze until she blushed and looked away. "I'd like to think you were hoping we could spend more time together."

"With Hana."

"Of course with Hana," he reassured her, "Like a proper family."

Beth's face lit with hope.

"That is what you want, isn't it?"

"More than anything in the world." She couldn't believe it. She couldn't believe Khal was telling her they could be together. But now his face had darkened, and Beth watched in concern as he stared without seeing into some place that gave him pain.

"The dust storm in the desert when I almost lost you…"

"Oh, Khal…" Remembering his confession about his sister, Beth realised Khal was not in a position to enjoy the type of joy she was feeling. Touching his arm, she stared into his face. "You saved my life, and I can never repay you."

He seemed surprised. "You don't owe me anything. If I'd lost you—"

"But you *didn't* lose me, I'm here. I'll always be here for you."

"I know you mean that."

"I do," Beth declared passionately. Khal, who had never revealed his feelings to anyone, was sharing them with her. She couldn't remember when she had felt so moved, or so full of love, apart from the moment when she'd first held Hana in her arms. And now her dreams had come true, and they were all going to be together like a proper family.

"Until the sandstorm I didn't realise how much you meant to me. I didn't realise what life would be like without you. And with Hana living here in the palace with us… My daughter, Hana." Khal's strong face softened momentarily. "Say you'll stay with me here in Q'Adar."

"You'd do this for us?" She searched his gaze. When she thought about all the difficulties Khal would have to face, and the criticism for taking a wife from such a very different background, she admired him even more. "You're serious about this, aren't you?"

"Never more so," he assured her firmly. "Hana and you are all I want. I didn't realise how far I would be prepared to go to ensure our future together. The events of last night have crystallised everything in my mind and helped me to see clearly where you're concerned."

"Oh, Khal…" Reaching up, Beth touched his face with her soft, warm hands. "You pretend to be so hard, but you're just like me, aren't you? We both have that empty space inside us that only one person can fill. It's recognising that person when they come along."

With Khal's love shining down on her, and Hana safe and well, Beth knew everything would be all right. She wasn't going to waste another minute worrying about the likelihood of a Liverpool shop-girl marrying the ruler of Q'Adar. She would just get on with it as she always did. She would take instruction from Khal and his advisors. She would learn the language and study the culture and history of Q'Adar. She would seek out charities she could champion and learn how best to help them. And, most important of all, she'd help Hana to understand the richness of her heritage from both sides of the world.

"So will you stay with me, Beth Tracey Torrance?" Khal asked her gently, bringing her in front of him. "Will you live with me and love with me?"

Trustingly holding his gaze, Beth whispered, "You know I will..."

He wanted to reward Beth for the courage she had shown during the sandstorm, and most of all for facing up to her new life in Q'Adar with such strong-minded determination. He wanted to give her a taste of what she could expect as his mistress in Q'Adar.

"What's this, Khal?" she said, her face lighting with surprise as he brought her into his private sitting-room. He had been impatient as she'd set-

tled Hana in her cot, having made these prepara-
tions earlier. He couldn't wait to see Beth's face
when she saw all the gifts he had for her.

"Are you excited?" he said as she stared at the
gift-wrapped packages. He realised she must be
overwhelmed, and wanted to reassure her as she
started opening them. "If the jewels aren't to your
taste, I can easily send for more—"

"More?" Beth breathed as she stared at him,
and then at the tumble of jewels falling through
her fingers. "Are these real?"

"Real? Of course they're real." He was pleased
with her reaction, and this was only the start.
Clapping his hands summoned a servant, who
brought a bronze casket and placed it on the table
where Beth was sitting. The man retired at his
signal and closed the door. Reaching inside the
pocket of his robe, he gave Beth a key. Instead of
pouncing on the casket as he had expected her to,
she frowned and turned the heavy old key over
in her hands. "Why don't you open the box instead of fiddling with the key?" he suggested. He
was impatient to move on to the next part of his
surprise, and had to stop himself taking the key
from her and opening the box himself.

He managed to restrain himself as she fumbled with the ancient lock. He noticed then that her hands were shaking, and tried to tell himself that excitement was the cause—but her face said something else. She looked apprehensive, which made him feel mildly irritated. He couldn't understand, when he was trying to give her all the things she'd never had, why she should be hesitating.

What did all this mean? Beth wondered. Hadn't she told Khal over and over again that he didn't need to buy her, and that she didn't want anything from him? An ugly suspicion had begun to take root in her mind, and that suspicion said Khal hadn't changed, and was using his wealth to tempt her to stay on in Q'Adar. When she had already agreed to do so, Beth thought, frowning.

She prayed she was wrong as she opened the lid of the old box. She stared inside, and didn't know whether to be relieved or not. There was nothing in it except for a bunch of keys and some photographs. "What are these?" she said, lifting them out. The photographs showed a very grand house that appeared to be in England. Set in parkland, there was a lake to one side of it, and a garden formally laid out at the front. She told herself it probably meant nothing, and that the wife of a sheikh would have to have a grand residence—even though all she wanted was Khal and Hana and a proper family, just as he'd promised her.

"House keys?"

Khal's lips curved. "Do you like it?"

"Is this our new residence in England?"

"I bought it for you, Beth."

"For me…" She should be thrilled, but her guts were twisting. "You mean we'll live here together?"

"You know I live in Q'Adar. It's for you whenever you want to return to England. I may visit you there from time to time. I don't ever want you to feel trapped here, Beth. That's why I bought it for you."

He made it sound as if they would live part of their lives completely independent of each other. Did married couples do that?

"Once you're under my protection, you'll have to have an appropriate residence in England."

Under his protection? Beth's apprehension grew. Were all her dreams about to come crashing down? She gazed at the discarded jewels on the table, and then at the photographs and keys.

"You made it clear you didn't like the penthouse," Khal went on when she looked to him for answers. "And so I bought you another property. You will need a garden, I can see that."

"A garden?" Beth's voice was shaking uncontrollably. "I need more than a garden, Khal."

"And you shall have more," he soothed. "You will have a home here in Q'Adar, as well as a mansion in Liverpool."

"But I don't want a mansion in Liverpool."

"I understand this has all come as a shock to you," Khal said indulgently. "But as my mistress you must get used to accepting gifts."

Shaking her head, Beth stumbled to her feet.

"And I want to give you the old fort too."

"Khal, please…" She held out her hands; they were shaking. "Please, stop this!"

"I thought you liked the old fort," Khal said, frowning. "I thought you were fascinated by its history—"

"I am!" Beth wailed, knowing if the stones had fallen down and buried her she couldn't have felt as bad as she did right now.

"Well, then?" Khal said, clearly thrown by her lack of enthusiasm.

This was not the tender lover she had known in the desert, the man who had sheltered her and saved her life. This was the ruler of Q'Adar, a man who expected his every wish to be a command, and who knew less than nothing about love.

"I'm determined to have the old fort renovated," he went on, as if oblivious to her torment. "And it will be good for you to take an interest in the project."

"Good for me?" Beth clutched her chest. "You never were talking about marriage, were you?"

"Marriage?" he said. "What are you talking about?"

"You must think I'm naïve," Beth said, unable to stem the tears pouring down her face. "You'd be right—I am naïve, and stupid too."

"Of course you're not stupid."

"I was making plans, Khal…I'd planned everything we'd do together when we were married, for Hana, and for Q'Adar…"

"You can still do these things; I don't see what's changed."

She laughed, a sad sound. "I'm wasting my time thinking there's a human being under those robes, aren't I? There isn't a human being behind your title, there's just the ruler of Q'Adar—a cold, unfeeling man." She shook him off when he tried to take hold of her. "A man who will stop at nothing to get what he wants, even if that means trampling over those who love him."

"Beth—"

"No, Khal!" She shook him off. "Did you think you could stick me away out of sight in the old fort so I'd be there at your convenience, and buy my silence with a holiday home in Liverpool? No!" she warned him again. "Stay away from me! You talked about love. You talked about how much I meant to you, when all the time you were planning this—"

"I was trying to show you how much you mean to me."

"By setting me up in a love nest at the old fort?"

"Eventually, when the renovations were completed, I did think we could meet there—"

"Far away from prying eyes?"

"I was thinking of you."

"And yourself too, no doubt!"

"I thought the renovation project would provide you with an ongoing interest."

"Don't you dare patronise me, Khal. I don't need anything to keep me busy. I'm a mother, I've got Hana, and I work for my living back in England."

"You can't just cut me out of your life," Khal reminded her.

"And you can't ignore mine. You have no idea, do you?" she exclaimed. "To you a relationship between a man and a woman is all about owner-ship and possession. For me, it's about the free-dom to love unconditionally—"

"And that's the difference between us," he cut across her. "I'm the realist, Beth, and you're the dreamer."

"And you dream of a warm bed and welcoming arms at the fort? No way, Khal! You can't stick me away in the desert and enjoy me whenever you have a spare moment."

"Don't make it sound so sordid."

"Isn't it?" She backed away from him, from his scent, from his heat, from his overwhelming presence. "What type of role models do you think we'd make for Hana if I do as you suggest?"

"Hana is a princess of Q'Adar, and will have an army of servants—"

"Hana doesn't *need* an army of servants, what she needs is love and security."

"And you think I wouldn't give her that?"

"I would never stop you seeing Hana, you know that, Khal. You also know I will never stay here as your mistress."

"I've only just got Hana back, and I won't let you take her out of Q'Adar."

"No court in the land would refuse you joint custody—"

"No court in which land?"

Beth shuddered involuntarily. The man she had so briefly known had disappeared, and she was confronting a stranger determined to impose his will on her. "Please don't be unreasonable. This is our daughter we're talking about."

"Exactly. Hana will live in the royal apartments, with me and with other members of the royal family."

Beth paled as the truth sank in. "And if you had your way Hana's mother would be housed some miles away, out of sight in the old fort? I don't think so."

He stopped her leaving at the door. "Where do you think you're going?"

"Away from you—to the nursery," Beth said as her thoughts came into clear focus. "I'm going to collect Hana, pack our cases, and get out of here—I'm going to take Hana home."

"This is her home, and if you want to go, if you want to leave without your daughter, so be it."

Beth could only stare at Khal in astonishment. "You can't mean that. You can't imagine I would leave without Hana?"

"Hana's place is in Q'Adar with me, as is yours."

"My *place*? Should I know my *place*, Khal? Is that it? Should I be grateful for all your bounty?" Beth cast a disparaging glance at the discarded jewels. "I've never known my place, and I can't be bought. Now, open this door," she said, rattling the handle. "Let me out of here!"

"You can go," he said, releasing his hold on the door. "But Hana stays with me."

"Stay with you? Do you think I want my daughter growing up with a stone for a heart? You think everything can be fixed with money and power, but I know it can't. I know when I'm being of-fered something worthless."

"Worthless? I'm offering you a home and security!"

"Shut away as your mistress?" When he remained silent, Beth shook her head. "It's an empty gesture, Khal. I already have a home, and Hana and I have everything we need."

"As a royal princess of Q'Adar, Hana will need round-the-clock security, can you give her that?"

Beth paled as the helplessness of her position sank in.

CHAPTER FIFTEEN

"It doesn't have to be like this," Khal told her as Beth turned her face from his blazing stare. "I never meant to hurt you. Beth, please listen to me. You shouldn't be so stubborn. You don't have to stand alone. You don't have to be brave all the time."

"Yes, I do."

As she bit her fist to stem the tears, he knew he ruled a country in which millions of people depended on him, but could see no way out of this. Having Beth stand broken in front of him was more than he could bear, and he would do anything to make it right for her. Anything except marry her, of course. He could never do that. "What can I do to make this better for you?"

"Nothing," she told him bluntly, recovering. "You can't do anything. Just let me appoint a lawyer who can help me sort this out."

"I can help you sort it out."

"I don't want your type of solution."

"We could live as a family here."

"Until you were married? I won't live some charade in Q'Adar, Khal."

"As my mistress you're not at risk," he said pragmatically. "You would be safe to return to the house in Liverpool whenever you wanted to."

"And leave Hana here with you and your bride?"

Folding his hands inside the sleeves of his robe, Khal stared at her levelly. "I suggest you go and think about this Beth...think about all your options."

She stared at him, the man she loved—a man so changed she hardly recognised him. "I'll do that, Your Majesty," Beth said tensely.

She had no intention of sitting around doing nothing, or of accepting her fate as decreed by His Majesty, Khalifa Kadir al Hassan. She rang the airport and booked a flight. It was that simple. Then she went to the nursery, and, after speaking to the staff on duty, lifted Hana from her cot. She had no intention of running off or sneaking away; she would do this properly. Hana wouldn't be at risk for an instant, because she would phone the Foreign Office in England and have the appropriate security measures put in place for when they landed. She had tried reason, but Khal wasn't interested, so now she would take action. Then later in England she would appoint a solicitor to act for them.

Beth asked one of the professional nannies to accompany her. "Just as far as the airport," she explained as they left the palace through a side gate. She had telephoned ahead to the coach house where there were drivers on duty night and day. "I want His Majesty reassured that Hana boarded the aircraft safely."

The woman assured her that she would do this, and Beth thanked her before climbing into the rear of the limousine with Hana asleep in her arms.

He guessed Beth would be in the nursery with Hana. When he discovered they were gone, he issued an all-points alert to close the borders. But if possible he intended to apprehend them himself. Beth's route was clear in his mind. She would try to take Hana back to England where she would feel safe. The controller on duty at the coach house confirmed this. The next thing he did was call up the limousine and tell the driver to return to the palace with his passengers immediately. When he'd done that, he'd jump in a Jeep to follow them overland while his helicopters circled overhead.

They had been driving for some time when Beth asked the driver to stop. He had been driving far too fast in Beth's opinion, and she was concerned for their safety on the bumpy road. She rapped on the glass when he didn't respond, and was alarmed when he ignored her.

"He's not our usual man," the nanny at her side told her. "I haven't seen him at the palace before."

"Great." Beth tightened her grip on Hana. Had she brought them all into danger? Now she knew why Khal had been so concerned. He hadn't wanted to frighten her, but she had gone about things in her usual stubborn way. If this was some clumsy kidnap attempt, then they were all in danger, even Khal. She had to warn him, and she must protect Hana and the nanny. But what could she do when she had no weapons to defend them, and wouldn't have known how to use them if she had? She was a stranger to the country and the driver could be taking them anywhere.

"He's taking the road to the border," the nanny whispered, as if reading her mind.

"Then we must stop him," Beth murmured back. All she knew was that they were in the wilderness somewhere between the palace and the airport. She rapped on the glass. When the man still ignored her, she resorted to panic measures. "I have to change the baby's nappy now!" Beth yelled down the intercom. "I can't do it on this bumpy road, so I suggest you stop unless you want a mess back here. Stop!" she said again, when he didn't answer. "I think my baby's ill. You'll be held responsible if anything happens to her!"

There was a second when the limousine didn't waver, and then the brakes went on, and it slewed terrifyingly from side to side before finally screeching to a halt.

"That stone memorial," Beth whispered to the nanny. "Can you see it? When we stop I want you to hide Hana under your clothes, and then make for those bushes. Don't run, just walk calmly, as if you want some privacy, and don't be distracted by anything." The woman was shaking, but Beth had to trust her now. "Keep Hana safe until I come for you." While she was talking, Beth was making a bundle of Hana's spare clothing, which she then wrapped in a shawl so it appeared she still had the baby. "My maid needs to relieve herself," she told the driver when he stopped the car.

"Good idea," he agreed, and got out too.

It was the best opportunity she was going to get. Taking the driver's seat, Beth gunned the engine, making for the stone memorial where she could see the nanny crouching down, hiding Hana. Beth's heart was hammering as she attempted to manoeuvre the big car but she wasn't used to driving on sand. The door snapped back on its hinges as the vehicle jerked forward, and then it careered across rocks and gullies until finally she lost control of the wheel and the tyres started to spin.

Leaping out, Beth could see the tyres were buried to the wheel-wells. There wasn't a chance she could manoeuvre the limousine out of the sand now.

He changed his mind about a Jeep and took a helicopter. That way he could reach the airport before the limousine and bring Beth and Hana back to the palace without fuss.

He gazed down, as he always did when he reached that part of the desert where his guilty past lay in a patch of sand—a reminder of mistakes he'd made in his youth, mistakes that could never be repaired. It was then that he saw something moving on the ground, and hovered lower.

Wading calf-deep in sand, Beth was cutting across some scrub-land, with Hana in one arm and her other arm around the nanny, urging her to move faster, when she heard the helicopter flying overhead. She couldn't lose time staring up at it to discover if it was friend or foe. Fear was draining her strength like water through a grid, and her chest felt about ready to explode. Risking a quick glance behind them, she saw their driver who had returned to the limousine flip open a mobile phone. They wouldn't be alone in the desert for long. She had been heading back to the road hoping to flag someone down. There wasn't much of a chance, but it was all she had.

* * *

He planted the big machine on the road between the on-coming truck and the fleeing women. Beth didn't know it, but she was heading straight into trouble. There wasn't time to land and pick them up safely, so he had opted to stop the insurgents first and hold them until his troops arrived. He carried guns onboard his helicopters and wouldn't hesitate to use them.

She stopped running when she saw the dust thrown up by the helicopter as it landed. The driver was back inside the limousine now, and with impatient stamps on the accelerator was trying to blast it out of the sand.

That should keep him busy, Beth thought, wiping her face on her sleeve. "Are you all right?" she asked the nanny, gazing intently at her charges. To her relief, Hana was sound asleep, but the young nanny was close to hysteria. She couldn't ask more of her, Beth realised, she'd asked too much already; she had to make their stand here. "We're going back to that memorial," she said firmly. "And I'm going to leave you there, hidden in the bushes, where you'll be safe while I get help."

"Don't leave me," the girl begged, clinging to her. "I have to go and get help. You can do this. I know you can." There were no certainties, but Beth wasn't about to share her fears. The only thing she did know was inaction wasn't an option.

Crouching low, Beth ran towards the helicopter. Seeing Khal standing outside was so much more than she had hoped for, her legs almost gave way beneath her, but, seeing the gun in his hand, she struggled on. It was a stark reminder that this was not a fairy story or a package tour to Q'Adar, but that it was a country in the throws of rebirth, with all that that entailed. Khal was a king, Sheikh of Sheikhs, a defender of his people. She just hadn't seen the big picture before. She had judged him as she would judge some nine-to-five worker, when in reality Khal was holding a country on his shoulders, and dealing with all the new emotions Hana had brought into his life at the same time. No wonder he seemed hard. He had to be.

Swinging the gun up, he shouted, "Beth! I could have shot you!" Grabbing hold of her, he hustled her towards the open door. "Get in now—don't ask questions!" He could see army trucks descending on them in a pincer movement. Time to leave. He had to keep Beth and Hana alive, whatever it took. "Where is she?"

"With her nurse in the bushes, by that memorial."

"We'll pick them up."

"And the driver?"

He angled his chin to the Sikorsky Black Hawk helicopters, flying fast and low across the sand to intercept the convoy. "They'll take care of him..."

It was a terrifying situation, but with Khal's hands steady on the controls Beth felt safe. She was seeing a new side to him. This was someone in another league to the entrepreneur who had built a business empire—this was a warrior king, a true hawk of the desert, a man playing out the hand fate had dealt him with a hero's instincts. Just like his ancestors before him, Khal would fight to keep his country safe. He would fight to keep his people safe, and those he loved too. The magnitude of his responsibilities had only just hit home. All the riches and outward show didn't mean a thing compared to the riches inside a man, and she felt a great swell of love for him, this man who was a protector, as well as the ruler of Q'Adar. Her part in his life seemed miniscule by comparison to the challenges he must face.

She mustn't be selfish, Beth thought, fighting the agony inside her; she must let him go when this was over. She clutched his arm, seeing they were hovering above Hana's hiding place. Fleetingly she wondered how she could have thought him unworthy to be a father, when he was the best father Hana could ever have.

"Here?" His voice sounded metallic through the headphones, but even so she heard the purpose in it.

"Yes."

He brought the helicopter swooping down.

"Bring her back to me safely—" But Khal had already gone. He'd barely landed the helicopter before he leapt out, and, ducking low beneath the deadly blades, sprinted away. She could do nothing now but wait tensely in her seat.

It was the longest few seconds of Beth's life, before air blasted into the cockpit and Khal was back with Hana in his arms and the young nanny clinging to him. Tears of relief poured down Beth's face when Hana was safe with her again.

Khal helped the young nanny into the back of the helicopter, seeing her safely strapped in with her headphones in place, before springing in next to Beth. There was no time to reassure her, he just hit some switches, grabbed the controls, and they lifted off.

The helicopter soared above the desert, leaving the drama below them to play out. Beth could see the insurgents had been captured by Khal's troops. Perhaps she had done some good, drawing them out into the open. She hardly knew. She was seeing things she had never dreamed of seeing—and she ached for Khal, understanding now more than ever the pressures he was facing as well. Knowing the trials ahead of him, she was frightened for him, and thought his position lonely as well as dangerous.

They landed on the roof of the palace, where they were instantly surrounded by support staff and armed guards. Having ensured they were taken care of, Khal hurried away. It was a relief for Beth to have so many practicalities to occupy her: taking care of Hana, reassuring the young nanny, allaying fears amongst her staff. Everyone was tense, and it was down to her to give them confidence in Khal's ability to handle the situation. She wasn't aware of her exhaustion, there was far too much to do.

He came to the nursery to check on Hana as soon as he could get away. Beth looked exhausted, and from the confident smiles and glances he received from her staff he guessed she hadn't rested for a moment since getting back. She was busy now, making sure the young nanny had access to a phone and the privacy to call her parents to reassure them. He waited while Beth took the girl to a small ante-room, where she left her to make the call. The dark circles under Beth's eyes were a reproach for him, and he only wished he could have saved her the distress she'd endured. "Beth…"

She looked at him distractedly for a moment. He could sense the adrenalin rushing through her veins, and knew the moment those levels dropped so would she. Then her eyes refocused, and relief flooded in. "Khal—are you all right?"

Always her first thought was for him. "I'm fine," he confirmed quickly. "Thanks to you, we've flushed out the last pocket of insurgents and captured their leader."

"I was wrong to put Hana at risk."

"No recriminations, Beth, what's the point?"

"How do you stand it?"

"Q'Adar is a country in a state of change, and will be for some time. This is my life, and these are my people. I'm not going to stop until corruption is driven out, and my people can enjoy the life they deserve."

"But not at the expense of *your* life."

"A country is more than one life, Beth, and if I can bring stability to Q'Adar the young people who follow me will take it forward."

"With you as their leader," she insisted stubbornly.

Rubbing a hand across his unshaven jaw, he looked at her. "What you did today was very brave."

She shrugged it off. "It was instinct, pure and simple. I was terrified."

"That's all right." He smiled grimly. "So was I. It's a foolish man indeed who doesn't know fear."

"I understand so much more now… About you, about Q'Adar."

"What are you saying, Beth?"

"Your people need you."

"And?"

"You always have been merciless in your need to know, Khal."

He relaxed slightly, shifting position. "That's how I survive."

Beth sensed the change between them. It was a change in understanding, and in the air. It was a change that wouldn't allow her to leave him, because she could only see that as the coward's way out now.

"Well?" he pressed again, raising his brows as he stared at her.

She drew herself up. "I need you." She held his gaze unflinchingly. "And, if you still want me to, I'll stay with you here, in Q'Adar, at your side."

For a moment he didn't move or respond in any way, and then with infinite slowness, so she could relish every tiny facial muscle softening, he began to smile. It was a smile of such tenderness and longing and humour and love—and warning, too, for all the difficulties that lay ahead of them. She hardly dared breathe in case she blinked and woke up, cold in bed somewhere without him.

The gap closed between them without either of

them being aware of moving, and as Khal seized Beth's hand, and brought it to his lips, he told her fiercely, "I don't deserve you."

CHAPTER SIXTEEN

THEY checked again on Hana and the young nanny before leaving the nursery, and then parted at the entrance to Beth's apartment, because Khal insisted she must rest.

"Take a bath," he suggested. "And then try to sleep for a while. I think you'll be surprised just how tired you are. If you wake in time, we'll have dinner together."

Of course she'd wake, Beth thought, wondering what all the fuss was about. She didn't want to part now like this, not when they'd been so close to sorting out the future. But as one of the maids opened the door to her, and acknowledged him with a respectful bow, Khal told the girl to make sure Beth didn't fall asleep in the bath.

"Honestly," Beth said, shaking her head. "You must think I'm a real weakling."

"Anything but," Khal said, sweeping his strong hands down his dusty jeans as he backed away.

"But now, if you will excuse me, I think we both need to listen to our bodies and take some rest."

"But I know you won't rest."

"I'll take a shower." His lips tugged up briefly in the vague approximation of a smile, and then he turned away.

Beth slept for so long and so soundly the maid had to shake her to wake her up.

"His Majesty has requested your presence at brunch."

"Brunch?" Beth said, scrambling up. "What time is it?"

Nearly noon the next day, Beth discovered with amazement. Taking a shower, she quickly changed into casual clothes, and then followed an attendant through the palace to the wing where the ruler of Q'Adar's private apartment was situated. She was taken through a plain-arched entrance to a part of the building that, like the man who lived there, was austere to the point of being spartan. The door that led the way into his office was a beautifully crafted, but undecorated mahogany. Khal was on the phone, and as the attendant left them, closing the door discreetly behind him, he beckoned her into the room. She could tell from his face he had something to tell her that she wouldn't like.

"You're safe to return home," he said.

Her brain emptied. Hadn't she agreed she would stay with him?

"I was just checking everything I've put in place for you is operational."

"But I thought—"

"I know what you said, and your offer touched me deeply, but you don't belong here, Beth, and it will be safe for you now in Liverpool. I have the co-operation of the British government. I don't want you to worry about a thing. I've even had my legal team identify three firms of solicitors for you to take your pick from—though, of course, you're free to go elsewhere if you prefer."

She couldn't answer him. Her stomach had turned to ice; her brain had stalled too. Only one question broke through. "And what arrangements have you made for your personal safety?" She despised the tremor in her voice.

"If I told you that, the arrangements wouldn't be secure, would they?"

Khal's lips quirked, but it was more than she

could do to respond to his battlefield humour this time.

"We're living in dangerous times, Beth, and there will always be greedy, ambitious men who put their own interest above my people. It's up to me to make sure they never take hold again, and it's also up to me to keep you safe."

"And Hana?"

"I'll drive you both to the airport first-thing tomorrow morning."

Beth was stunned. "You're letting Hana go?"

"It's wrong to keep a child from its mother. And, now I know a personal-protection squad has been detailed to mount a round-the-clock watch on her, I'm reassured."

And it was wrong to take a child from a father who adored her, but as usual Khal was making sacrifices for the good of other people. She had done a lot of growing up since coming to Q'Adar, Beth realised, and Khal had taken a long journey too. Was there any greater gift he could have given her than this?

They drove to the airport the following morning in silence. There were outriders and several more cars containing armed men behind them. This was Khal's life, and she was leaving him to get on with it. She was deserting him in the middle of a situation that, whatever he said to reassure her, Beth knew still had time to run. She glanced sideways at Khal's strong, resolute face beneath his traditional headdress, knowing he would steel himself to this parting from Hana as he steeled himself to so many things.

She knew all too well what it was like to have no one in whom you could confide, and Khal was in exactly the same position. For all the apparent strength and closeness of his family, he had always protected them from the truth. As sole ruler of Q'Adar, he wouldn't share his innermost thoughts with anyone. How sad and ridiculous that their different stations in life meant they could never be close, when they were so alike in so many ways. They had so much to offer each other, and all of that was to be wasted.

With a deep sigh, she turned to stare out of the windows at the harsh realities of a land undergoing change. But, even with all the upheaval she had experienced first-hand, she could see new Artesian wells, reflecting Khal's remorseless quest for water to feed his new crops. And even with her personal preoccupations she couldn't help smiling and pressing her face against the window to wave to a group of children who had gathered to watch the passing cavalcade. Khal's responsibilities seemed endless to her, and even with a council to help him he would make all the final decisions, decisions that would affect the future of all the children of Q'Adar.

They were shown into the VIP lounge where there was no possibility of Khal speaking privately with her, or even showing the affection towards Hana which Beth was certain he longed to do. However comfortable the lounge, it seemed a sterile place to say goodbye to someone you loved. There were so many people waiting to greet him, and as always Khal made each one of them feel special. He could be gracious and gentle and genial, with his warrior self completely hidden. But it was always duty for him—duty first, duty always, even now. No wonder his people loved him and trusted him to bring them the settled existence they had so longed for.

He came over at last and addressed himself first to the female bodyguard to whom he had entrusted Beth and Hana's safety. "Take good care of them," he said, glancing at Beth. As the woman assured Khal that she would, Beth held Hana closer, hoping beyond hope she had the courage to keep her dignity while Khal bowed to her in the traditional Arabian salutation before turning to go. She swallowed hard on her tears as he strode from the room, followed by his attendants. She felt instantly empty and lost. Her lover, her heart, had gone; half of her had been ripped away—the better half.

He took the small, fast car they had brought to the airport for him to drive, and pushed it to the limit along the seemingly endless desert road. He didn't want to think. He didn't want anything, or anyone. He needed space and privacy to lick his wounds like an injured animal. The pain of parting from Beth and Hana was unendurable. He had dismissed his bodyguards and outriders and now he needed only one companion—and she was lying deeply buried in the sand beneath her monument.

The Ferrari slewed to a halt in a spray of sand. Backing up carefully, he parked it at the edge of the stony track along which Beth had led her tiny group to safety. But he hadn't come to relive those memories, but to remember his sister and her bright, humorous eyes.

Those same eyes had held his gaze when she'd challenged him to exchange horses with her so she could prove herself the better rider. He'd been young and full of thoughtless energy then. He had laughed at her suggestion, and had sprung down readily from his mount. She'd had the better horse. He'd known it, and had longed to test it. It was a far faster horse than his, and though she'd pressed his stallion hard his sister had fallen behind him. He had been so suffused with triumph he'd punched the air, unaware that the desert had taken her. She had tried to cut him off and had veered from the track. She had been lost, sucked down into the treacherous quicksand, a silent and terrible death.

Since then he had never shared his thoughts with anyone, and had been closed off to feelings. He had embraced the responsibilities of Q'Adar with relief, if only because it had meant he would never have time to feel anything ever again. He had been so certain it would be enough and would bring him ease, but nothing could be further from the truth. He knew now that he only had one life, and must live it to the full as his sister had. He had always respected Ghayda's passion for life, and this half-life of his would have angered her, and did no honour to her memory. He had been so foolish, so blinkered and narrow-minded...

Resting his hand on the weathered stone, he watched the giant aircraft taking Beth and Hana home soar into the sky above his head. "I love you," he whispered to his sister, and to Beth.

Normally she felt a little glow of pleasure each time she slipped the key into the lock of her very own home. Growing up in a series of featureless institutions had made her intensely territorial, Beth supposed. But today she felt empty. Picking up the Moses basket, she carried Hana into the hallway and shut the door. The adventure was over. They had made a clean break from Khal at the airport, and now she had to get used to life without him.

She made a determined effort to force back tears when Faith emerged from the kitchen.

"What a wonderful surprise!" Beth exclaimed with genuine pleasure. "I can't tell you how glad I am to see you. Does this mean your father's better?"

"Yes, it does," Faith confirmed, giving Beth and Hana a joint hug.

It made things bearable. She needed friends around her to fill the empty spaces, though in her heart Beth knew those spaces would never be filled.

"Shall I take Hana upstairs for you and settle her?" Faith offered.

"I'll make us both a cup of tea while you do that," Beth said, tenderly handing Hana over. She thought Faith looked happier than she had in a long time, and put it down to the worry about her father no longer troubling her. But Beth's smile faded the moment Faith and Hana were out of sight. She would never get used to life without Khal in it.

She made a pot of tea and then walked, pensively nursing her mug, into the sitting room... where she almost dropped it. "Khal?" Her lungs contracted, and she had to steady herself with her hand on the back of the sofa. "How on earth?"

"Did I get here before you?" he said, moving out of the shadows. "I cheated."

Even in Western clothes he was an incongruous sight in the small, neat room.

"Well, Beth… Aren't you going to say hello?"

The crease was back in his cheek, she noticed, and his gaze warmed her frozen lips. "Hello," she said foolishly. "How?"

"You were in a lumbering passenger plane with a two-hour check in."

"While you were piloting your own fast jet, and had VIP clearance." she finished for him. She was just an ordinary girl in an extraordinary situation, Beth realised as Khal smiled faintly in agreement.

The crease in his cheek deepened. "What's a jet between friends, Beth?"

"Friends…"

"I hope so."

"Why are you here?" She spoke in a very small voice, not sure she wanted to hear the answer.

"Because we have unfinished business. And because I want you back," he said after a moment.

"I can't… Not again—"

"Hear me out. I need you in Q'Adar. The country needs you."

"Q'Adar needs me?" she said frowning.

"Wasn't it you who said that a country is more than a balance sheet?"

"But I'm an outsider; I don't know how to help."

"You told me you had plans... The nursery, remember? And that was just the start, you said. You told me a country needs a heart. You are that heart—or you could be, if you wanted to be. And remember, I spent all my school years and most of my adult life out of the country, so I'm a stranger too. But I went back to Q'Adar, and I'm glad I did. The country needs strong leadership, Beth, or it will descend into chaos."

"I wouldn't fall apart," she said, eyes growing misty as she allowed herself to share Khal's dream for a moment.

"I know that. I also remember something else you said: a country needs more than strong leadership, it needs a human face."

"But not *my* face."

"Aren't you Beth Tracey Torrance? Aren't you the same girl who turned my world upside down?

Well, Beth? Have you nothing to say? Have I found a way to silence you at last?"

"Maybe... Maybe you have," Beth agreed.

Taking hold of her hands, Khal brought them to his lips. "I'm asking you to come back with me...for good, this time. I know it can't be an easy decision for you, and I know I've been selfish and blinkered."

"No," she argued fiercely. "You're a man who became a king, a man thrown out of his world into a dangerous situation, where you must work against the clock to bring order to Q'Adar or be destroyed in the attempt."

"You're so wise, little Beth."

"Not so much of the little, if you don't mind," she said, gathering her Liverpool spirit around her. As they stared at each other, they both found it hard to hold back the warmth and relief in their eyes that said they were sharing the same space again.

"Beth Tracey Torrance, I love you," Khal said, holding her gaze. "And I always will, whether you agree to come back with me or not."

"You really mean that, don't you?"

His shoulders eased in an accepting shrug. "Fate means us to be together."

"Fate didn't take account of my terms," she interrupted pragmatically.

"No, but I did…"

She paused and grew serious. "What are you saying, Khal?"

"I'm saying I let you go once before, and I will never do that again. I'm saying that I want you at my side always, and that I will meet your terms in order to achieve that."

"But how?" Beth bit down on her lip, wanting to believe life could give them a break. But how could it, when Khal was a king and she was no one, and when she wouldn't, she couldn't, sacrifice her principles?

"If I can't live without you, what do you suggest we do?" Khal said.

Beth made a gesture of helplessness. "I give up."

He smiled. "Now, that's not like you."

"I know I couldn't live close by you in Q'Adar and see you with another family, your official family. It would break my heart."

"My official family?" He cut across her. "Beth,

you and Hana *are* my family." Closing his eyes, Khal spoke her name as if he wanted to brand it on his soul. "You don't know how much I love you," he said.

"Not enough to sacrifice your country, and I wouldn't ask you to."

"All I need from you is to know you feel the same way I do."

"You know I do," Beth said passionately. "I can't live without you, but I must. However hard we wish for things, we can't always have what we want."

"Why can't we?" Khal demanded, bringing Beth's hands to his lips.

"It's just not our fate, our karma—"

"Rubbish!" Khal said fiercely. "Show me a perfectly smooth path where love is concerned and I'll believe in miracles!" Cupping her chin, he made her look at him. "Don't let me down now, Beth Tracey Torrance."

"I don't have an answer for you."

"But I have a question for you."

"Tell me," she said, ready to help him in any way she could.

"Will you marry me, Beth? Will you give your heart to me, and to Q'Adar?"

Beth's lips worked, but no sound came out. She tried to fathom it in her mind. She couldn't. "So Beth Tracey Torrance, of no known background, can marry His Majesty Khalifa Kadir al Hassan, Sheikh of Sheikhs, Bringer of Light to his People in Q'Adar?" she said at last.

"We can marry wherever you like," Khal said dryly.

"You're serious, aren't you?"

"Of course I'm serious. Why do you doubt me?"

"Because the picture you paint is not only improbable, it's impossible," Beth said sensibly.

"Who says it's impossible?"

Beth shook her head as Khal drew himself up. "Well, clearly not you, Your Majesty."

"So, why doubt yourself?" Khal demanded.

"Because I'm no one."

"No one?" Khal laughed as he stared down at her.

"You can't just laugh this off," Beth protested. "The whole world will know that I'm a shop girl from Liverpool who came to the desert and fell in love with a sheikh—they'll say I'm your plaything."

"Not when you're my wife."

"They'll say I slept with you and had your baby."

"Do I care?" Khal interrupted. "Do you care what people say?"

"I care what they say about you. It's so undignified."

Khal's lips tugged. "Loving you is *undignified*?"

"They'll say I got pregnant on purpose."

"They can say what they like and be deeply envious. You can't have that much fun without getting pregnant."

"Khal, please, this is serious—"

"No one will say anything derogatory about you in my hearing. We love each other, and that's enough. I never took you for someone who would crumble if people said unkind things about you, and I still can't imagine you allowing your life to be governed by what other people think. So if that's all that's holding you back, Beth— Or are you afraid at the thought of life with me?"

"No!"

"I understand if you are," he said. "I hope the dangerous times are over in Q'Adar, but there are no guarantees."

"I can't expose Hana to ridicule." Beth bit her lip as imaginary newspaper-headlines unfolded in her mind.

"Hana won't be exposed to anything unpleasant when we're married. I'd rather have someone true and honest and real at my side than any princess you care to name. I know I'm asking a lot of you, Beth. If you marry me you're condemning yourself to a life in the spotlight, but when the world sees you as I do, and realises how wonderful you are…"

"Beth Tracey Torrance, Queen of Q'Adar?" Cocking her head to one side, Beth stared at Khal incredulously.

"You don't see yourself as I do. You're like a breath of fresh air, and you have so much to give. You're the only person who remains to be convinced, Beth. You're never going to please everyone, so don't even try. Just do what you know to be right. And this *is* right, you know it is."

"I'll bring you down."

"Bring me down?" Khal looked at Beth. Far

from bringing him down, she lifted him up. "Strength isn't centred in wealth and power, it's in here, Beth." He touched his heart. "I need your strength, as you need mine. I'm so much more with you than I can ever be without you. You make me feel, and you make me see things differently. You give me love and laughter, and an enthusiasm for life. You took the black and white of my world and painted it in vivid colours. You make me hurt and wish and long and hope... You gave me Hana," he finished softly.

As Khal's arms closed around her, Beth saw his tears, and was even more astonished when he knelt at her feet. "Beth Tracey Torrance... Will you do me the honour of becoming my wife?"

"It can be a quiet wedding," Beth suggested, now she was starting to plan something in her mind that had always seemed impossible. "No one needs to know except us. And I'll stay in the background when we're married—" Seeing the expression in Khal's eyes, she broke off. "What?"

"That's not what I have planned for you at all."

That irresistible crease was back in his cheek, Beth noticed. "What have you got up your sleeve?" she demanded as Khal stood up and embraced her.

"You'll have to wait and see. But far from hiding you away I have something quite different in mind. When I show off my beloved wife, and our precious baby daughter, the whole world is going to know."

Just as Khal had promised, the world's press had assembled for the wedding of His Majesty Khalifa Kadir al Hassan to Beth Tracey Torrance from Liverpool. And as the ceremonial horn of Q'Adar sounded, the Nafir, made out of copper with its single piercing note—Beth hurried to the window to enjoy the sight of the Sheikh of Sheikhs" loyal subjects gathered in a tented city that housed hundreds of thousands of people on the vast desert plain

"You look absolutely beautiful," Khal's mother told her, as she made the final adjustments to Beth's gauzy veil.

Then Faith carried Hana up to Beth for a kiss, and as Hana crowed with happiness the three women shared a conspiratorial glance. Only they and Khal knew that Beth and Khal were already married; a small, private ceremony for just the two of them with plain wedding bands and no guests, other than Faith and Khal's mother, who had acted as their witnesses. The rest was between Beth and Khal and the fate that had brought them together. But this grand wedding was at Khal's insistence. They didn't need the pomp and ceremony, but he wanted to show Beth off to the world, and to his people…

Her people now, Beth thought, gazing out of the window at the kingdom she loved. Her gaze lingered on the mountains and the monument in front of them where she had gone earlier that morning with Khal, just the two of them on horseback, to lay her wedding flowers as a wreath of remembrance and love on his sister's grave. She sensed it had been a cathartic moment for Khal, and had brought them even closer together.

And now the time had come and, surrounded by those who loved her, Beth walked out of her apartment and along the corridors to the top of the grand marble staircase in the Palace of the Moon, where she looked down on the crowded assembly. Her gaze locked instantly with Khal's, and in response to his look of love she started her journey towards him.

EPILOGUE

THREE months earlier Khal had bought an emergency licence. For an emergency marriage, he'd told Beth, dragging her into his arms to tease her with kisses.

"You can't do that in Liverpool," she'd protested, leaping up in bed in her little house.

"If the Sheikh of Sheikhs can't, then he'll find someone who will."

"Friends in high places?"

"Relations between our two countries have never been better," Khal had agreed, throwing Beth down on the pillows. "I've got something for you."

"What is it?" she demanded, starting to rifle the pockets of his casual jacket.

"This," he said, straight-faced, handing her a box he had hidden behind his back. "I know you can't stand jewellery."

"Who says I can't?"

"And so I thought..."

"Khal," Beth protested, leaping up in bed. "What have you done?" She burst out laughing as he opened the ornate jewellery box and plucked out the "engagement ring" he'd bought her.

"Plastic fantastic!" she exclaimed. "How did you know it's exactly what I wanted? Did you have it made especially for me?" Holding it up to the light, she brandished the chunky ring, pretending to admire it.

"I had to buy a lot of crackers before I found one I thought you'd like."

"I love it, and I'll never take it off," she assured him, over-acting terribly.

"I hope you don't mean that," Khal said, turning serious. "It could give a man a nasty bruise."

"And what's this?" Beth said, as he handed her an intact cracker.

"Let's pull it and see, shall we?" he suggested, joining her on the bed.

Beth gave it all she'd got, and gasped when the contents came tumbling out. "Is this real?" she gasped.

"Please, not that again," Khal begged her, affecting weariness.

"Okay, it's real," Beth agreed excitedly. "But Khal, you shouldn't have."

"Okay, give it back to me."

"No—finder's keepers…"

"Let me help you, then," he said, easing the plastic ring from Beth's wedding finger and re-placing it with the most spectacular jewel Beth had ever seen. The ring was composed of a cluster of sapphires in all the colours of the rainbow."

"Except for red," Khal explained. "Because red is the preserve of the ruby…"

"Oh, Khal, no!" Beth protested when he brought out yet another ring from his shirt pocket. "You can't do this."

"Who says?" he demanded. And now he replaced the second ring with a third, a ruby heart the size of a quail's egg.

Beth was astounded. She had never seen anything like it. The ruby heart was surrounded by the most fabulous blue-white diamonds.

"I hope you like it." Khal said dryly. "You can keep the plastic for every day."

"I love it…"

"Good," he said, and, ignoring laughing protests, he brushed the debris off the bed, threw off his clothes, and joined her beneath the covers.

* * *

The grand ceremony in the Palace of the Moon was quite a wedding, though they both knew that nothing could mean as much to them as that simple service back in Liverpool. The two weddings had reflected their very different lives, but from now on they would walk the same path, and share the same life...

Khal had been waiting for her, looking magnificent in his robes of Bedouin black trimmed with the crimson and gold of the al Hassan family, while Beth's fairy-tale gown had been picked out for her by her friends at the Khalifa store in Liverpool. She was going to keep in contact with all of them, now Khal had involved her in the business—though her brief had just expanded to embrace a country. For, when Khal placed the official wedding-band of Q'Adar on her finger, she became queen of that country. That ring would sit next to the plain gold wedding-ring he had bought for her in Liverpool, and in tribute to both their countries she would never take either ring off.

It seemed for ever that day until they were alone again. "You didn't need to do all this for me,"

Beth protested, staring out across the ocean as Khal's yacht slipped out of port. Their honeymoon would be brief but wonderful, as neither of them could bear to be parted from Hana for longer than a few days. Of course Beth wasn't to know that Khal had arranged for Hana and Faith to join the yacht when they docked at the next port. It was just one of many surprises the ruler of Q'Adar had planned for his beloved wife.

"I know I didn't have to do anything for you," he said. "Which is why I want to do so much for you."

As Khal moved to brush her hair back from her face when the ocean breeze tossed it in her eyes, Beth trapped his hand in hers. "Well, I'm very glad you did…"

"So am I…" He turned her hand and stared down at the ring she was wearing. "The colours of the sapphire will always remind us that life is full of possibility."

"If we take it by the scruff of the neck and shake it?" Beth suggested with a laugh.

"I couldn't have put it better myself—though right now that's not what I've got in mind…" He glanced towards the companionway that led the way to the owner's suite.

"So it's more of a passionate ruby-red-heart sort of moment?" Beth guessed, smiling up at him.

"Exactly," Khal agreed, drawing Beth into his arms.

* * * * *